Our soul waiteth for the Lord:
he is our help and our shield.
—*Psalm* 33:20

For my sister Heather: I wouldn't trade our unconventional Alaskan childhood for anything. I'm thankful we shared it together.

Chapter One

Today she'd make Rex Adams an offer on his property he couldn't refuse.

Eliana Madden studied her landlord over the rim of her coffee mug as he claimed the last vacant stool at the counter in the Harbor Lights Café, the business she'd poured every ounce of herself into since she started waiting tables here over ten years ago.

When the previous managers had retired and moved to California, she'd boldly approached Rex and his wife, Tammy, and asked to manage the café. No one had been more surprised than her when they'd offered her the position. People in Hearts Bay as well had believed in her, a twentysomething recent college graduate with zero management experience. The customers' loyalty meant everything, and she wouldn't have succeeded without them. Now if only she could convince Tammy and Rex to finally sell her the business.

If they'd accept her offer for the building and the property, she'd be able to get started on her renovation plans instead of submitting frequent maintenance requests for the leaky roof and cranky old water heater.

Rex and Tammy were formidable obstacles standing between her and her dream of owning the café. Their families had been arguing for years over who deserved to own this swath of waterfront property in Hearts Bay, Alaska.

She couldn't let that bitter conflict discourage her, though.

The bell on the front door jangled as more customers filed in, pulling her from her thoughts. It was time to put her plan into action.

The café hummed with the usual weekday morning crowd. Outside the wall of windows spanning the far side of the dining room, a light rain was falling. Fog had draped its lazy fingers around the masts of the boats in the harbor and languished over the water surrounding Orca Island. Voices filled the air, silverware scraped across plates and the aromas of coffee and eggs mingled. There wasn't an empty seat in the whole place.

An unexpected tightness made her throat ache. If her brother, Charlie, were here, he'd lean one elbow on the worn Formica countertop and tell her to go for it. He'd also be the first to show up and help blow out the side wall and add more seating. He used to eat breakfast at the café all the time. Third stool from the end. She avoided sitting there after hours and only served the customer in that seat if no one else was available. She'd secretly entertained thoughts of removing it in honor of her late brother, but that seemed a little over-the-top, even for her.

This week marked two years since he'd been gone. A fishing boat accident had killed him and Abner, her sister Mia's fiancé.

Man, she missed them.

"Order up." Anthony, the line cook, pushed an omelet with a side of bacon through the service window.

Eliana set down her yellow mug with the café's logo printed in blue letters and wiped her suddenly clammy palms on the blue apron tied around her waist.

"Kelly, will you take this to Jim at table three, please? There's someone here I need to speak to."

"Of course." Kelly grabbed the plate and strode toward Jim, her strawberry blond ponytail bobbing against her sunshine-yellow T-shirt. The woman was a gift. Always on time and happily picked up extra shifts whenever anyone asked her to cover for them.

Anthony caught her eye through the service window and winked. "Go get 'em, boss."

Eliana flashed him a wobbly smile. Her sneakers felt like they were loaded with mud as she inched along her side of the L-shaped counter. Anthony had found her in the pantry this morning, praying about how to convince Rex to let her buy him out. When Anthony praised her bravery, she'd almost believed him.

More like a foolish girl with a pie-in-the-sky idea. She didn't feel brave. Not with the mayor, two town council members and her middle school basketball coach eating their breakfasts at the counter. All lined up. Right next to Rex.

With his short-cropped dark hair graying at the temples, brow permanently furrowed from years spent on his flying bridge, guiding countless fishing charters through the unpredictable waters off the island's coast, and facial features that reminded her of a bald eagle, he'd always made her nervous. While he thankfully hadn't passed that stern expression onto his sons, the gray-blue eyes reminded her so much of Tate that it physically hurt to look at Rex.

She'd always imagined Rex would someday be her father-in-law. Her babies' grandpa. Someone she'd eat Sunday dinners with from now until forever. Instead, they barely spoke unless they had café related business to discuss, and she couldn't remember the last time she'd been in his house.

Rex paused, his coffee mug halfway to his mouth. Whatever conversation he'd been having with Mr. Struthers, the local fish and game warden, screeched to a halt when Eliana hovered in front of them.

"Good morning." She tried for a casual greeting. Her cheeks immediately flamed when her words came out almost an octave higher than normal.

Not to mention earning curious stares from at least six of the twelve people at the counter, who had all angled their heads to listen in. Orca Island had about eight thousand residents and less than fifty miles of highway from one end to the other. All the news traveled quickly through the community of Hearts Bay and beyond. Even folks in the outlying villages, who needed a plane or a boat to get to town, didn't have to wait long to hear the latest and greatest updates.

"Hello, Eliana." The crevices in Rex's forehead deepened. His piercing gaze drilled into her. "Something I can help you with?"

"Actually, yes." She tipped her chin up and drew a ragged breath. "I want to make an offer on the café. The building, the business and the land."

Rex frowned. The sound of silverware scraping across plates faded into the background. Her heart climbed into her throat.

Just answer me.

"You're too late. A developer from Portland already made an offer. He wants to build a luxury hotel with a convention center. We're signing the paperwork next Friday."

"I'm sorry to hear that." She slunk away like a fox with its tail tucked between its legs, outsmarted once again.

Next Friday was only ten days from now. Eliana felt the weight of Anthony's sympathetic gaze as she picked up two plates of pancakes, then plastered on a smile and delivered the food to her customers at a table by the window. Rex's words had poured gasoline on the flames of resentment kindling in her abdomen.

A luxury hotel and convention center?

What a horrible idea. The modern steel-and-glass facility she envisioned would ruin Hearts Bay's pristine coastline. She wasn't interested in prolonging the dispute over this land, but she refused to sit back and let Rex and Tammy crush her dreams. She had to find a way to stop them from closing the deal with the developer.

Dumbest decision ever.

Two flights, one sleepless night in a cheap hotel, plus a ten-hour ferry ride across an angry ocean with four-year-old twins had left Tate Adams dangling at the end of his single-dad rope.

Holding his breath, he shoved Hunter's soiled T-shirt into a plastic bag he'd begged the attendant in the dining room to give him. Willow and Hunter clung to his legs as he stood near their seats in the ferry's front cabin, trying desperately to keep them calm until they docked at Hearts Bay.

The poor kids had battled seasickness almost the entire trip. They couldn't even keep down the chewable medication an empathetic passenger had offered.

Adams, you're an idiot. So much for giving Willow and Hunter an authentic Alaskan experience. When Jade, his ex-wife, had begged him to care for their twins for the entire summer, he'd agreed, *if* she allowed him to bring the kids to Orca Island. He'd been so excited to come home he hadn't considered that taking the longest route possible from Boise might be too much for his landlubbers to handle.

"Daddy, I want out." Willow pointed out the rain-spattered window. "Let's go watch for whales."

"It's raining, pumpkin." Tate tried and failed to peel Hunter off his leg. Poor kid. He still looked green. And miserable.

"We can wear our new raincoats." Willow plucked her shiny white jacket with pink polka dots off the vinyl chair nearby. "Put yours on, too, Hunter."

"No." Hunter shook his head and tightened his grip on Tate's leg. "I don't want to."

Both kids had their mother's unruly golden curls. Willow's hair skimmed her shoulders, while her twin brother's flopped over his forehead. They looked like they hadn't seen a comb in days.

"The fresh air might make you feel better." Tate reached for Hunter's lime-green coat with the frog face on the back. "We'll come back inside if you get too cold."

"I won't get cold." Willow shoved her feet into the bright pink rain boots she'd discarded earlier. "Hurry, Hunter. I want to see a whale."

"Fiinnne." Hunter dragged the single syllable word out, complete with a dramatic eye roll.

Splendid. Must've learned that from Jade.

An older woman sitting in the row of chairs nearby shot Tate an amused glance. He pretended not to notice and wrangled Hunter into his coat and green rain boots.

"Let's go." Willow skirted around the row of chairs, then hurried toward the door.

"Wait for us, please," Tate called over his shoulder. The girl had no fear. He couldn't let her leave the cabin alone.

Hunter clutched Tate's hand. "What if I throw up again?"

Tate gently guided him away from his seat. "You're not going to throw up."

Please, Lord, don't let him be sick anymore.

They crossed the cabin, and Tate opened the door. Willow scrambled out onto the deck while Hunter hung back. The captain had slowed down. They glided through the emerald-green water at a snail's pace. Frigid air enveloped them as Tate clasped Willow's and Hunter's hands in his and led them toward the railing near the bow.

Rain pattered their faces. Willow tipped her head back and squealed with delight. Hunter glued himself to Tate's side. Poor little fella.

"Look." Tate pointed to the snowcapped mountain rising out of the gray mist. "That's Mount Larsen, the tallest point on the island."

"Can we climb it?" Willow pressed up on her toes, one hand gripping the ferry's railing.

Tate chuckled. "We can't climb to the top. There's a hiking trail and an observation deck. By the way, your great-grandmother was a Larsen. That mountain is named after—"

"I'm cold." Hunter shivered. "Can we go in?"

"But I haven't seen any whales yet." Willow's brows scrunched together. "Where are they, Daddy?"

Oh, boy. Tate swallowed an impatient sigh. It was going to be a long summer. He squeezed their hands and breathed in the familiar briny scent he'd always associated with home. *Home.* After being away for almost eight years, he'd never imagined he'd return as a single dad with twins. Life hadn't gone at all like he'd planned. Even though he regretted his failed marriage, Willow and Hunter were tremendous blessings. He hoped and prayed this trip would soothe their hurt and confusion over not seeing their mother for three months.

"Is that Grandpa Rex's boat?" Willow pointed to a commercial fishing boat chugging past the ferry.

The *Matilda Jean.* Charlie Madden's boat. Tate's chest tightened. "No, honey. That's a seiner. It's made for catching thousands of pounds of salmon. See the nets?"

He pointed to the black nets suspended from the boat's massive gray rigging. Her white bow sliced through the blue-green water. The black stripe and hand lettering on the boat's stern flooded Tate with memories of Eliana, her family and everything they'd lost when Charlie died.

Tate should've come home for the funeral. He'd wanted to. But the twins had been a challenge that summer, and his marriage had started to crumble. Besides, he'd been too ashamed to face Eliana. Their friendship had meant a lot to him. He'd felt guilty that he'd married someone Eliana had never met. Not that he needed her blessing or anything, but best friends usually attended each other's weddings. He hadn't even invited Eliana. Frankly, he'd been a coward. Let his family influence his choices, and then he'd convinced himself that Jade was the ideal woman for him.

"Then where's Grandpa's boat?" Hunter asked.

"We can't quite see the boats in the harbor yet." He released Willow's hand and gestured toward Hearts Bay's ferry terminal visible in the distance. "That's where the ferry will dock in a few minutes."

Hunter's blue eyes welled with unshed tears. "Do I have to get on Grandpa's boat today?"

Tate dropped to one knee on the deck. Water soaked the fabric of his jeans. He pulled Hunter into his arms. "Buddy, you're safe with me. You don't have to ride on Grandpa Rex's boat if you don't want to. I promise we'll have lots of fun together, even if we stay on land."

Hunter buried his face in the Gore-Tex fabric of Tate's jacket. His little body trembled. Tate squeezed his eyes shut. *What have I done?*

"Where are we going to live?" Willow tapped her boot in a puddle of water pooling on the deck. "With Grandma and Grandpa?"

Hunter pulled away and swiped the back of his hand across his cheeks. "What does our house look like?"

"I'll show you when we get there." Tate stood, keeping one hand on Hunter's shoulder. "It's a two-story building overlooking the harbor. In a few minutes, you'll be able to see its blue metal roof. Our apartment is upstairs, above Grandpa Rex's fishing charter office."

And right beside the café that Eliana managed. His mother had mentioned that at least twice when he'd called to discuss his summer plans. He and Eliana hadn't seen one another in years, but he still hadn't forgiven himself for ending their friendship when he'd moved to Idaho. Maybe he'd be so busy with the twins and helping Dad with his fishing charters that they'd rarely cross paths.

Maybe she'd married by now and started a family of her own.

The notion doused him with another wave of regret. Ugh. He had really messed up.

"Who will watch us when you go fishing?" Hunter stared up at him. Tears still clung to his dark eyelashes.

The fear in his son's eyes pierced Tate's heart. "Don't worry. I've hired a babysitter, but it's going to be a while until I need her to watch you."

Hunter quirked his mouth to one side. "How long is a while?"

"Check it out—we're almost to the dock." He redirected Hunter's attention to the long wooden pier jutting out into the ocean. Seagulls lined the edge, like an unofficial welcoming committee.

Crew members hustled to their duty stations. A woman in a yellow raincoat stood at the end of the dock, waiting to disembark passengers and vehicles. The vessel creaked and groaned, churning up water as it eased into position.

Willow peppered Tate with more questions while Hunter got quiet, the weight of the world blanketing his slumped shoulders. The more Willow danced around, her body humming with excitement, the more Hunter shrank into the fear of the unknown.

This summer was supposed to be about healing. About spending time with his family and showing his children the beauty of Alaska.

But he couldn't shake the ominous feeling that he'd made a mistake when he'd agreed to let Jade shirk her parenting responsibilities and focus on her new husband. Her absence had plunged Hunter into a tailspin. What if he never recovered?

* * *

Tate was here.

Eliana stood frozen in front of the café, clutching her tote bag with the bank deposit inside, her mouth gaping wide enough to park a snowplow inside.

This couldn't be happening. Not only had Rex Adams delivered the crushing news that he was a sellout, he'd also failed to mention his son was coming home. Or that he was bringing two of the world's most beautiful children to visit. The wheels of Tate's suitcases hummed over the asphalt, and a boy and girl with shocks of honey-blond curls trailed behind him. They wore shiny raincoats and adorable boots and towed tiny suitcases.

She let her gaze slide past them, expecting Tate's wife to stroll out of the mist like a supermodel on a Paris runway. Because Tate's wife did in fact look like a supermodel. Eliana had acquired this information during an unfortunate late-night deep dive into Tate's social media. The evidence of his perfect life—the one he'd built without her in Idaho—was all there in cute snapshots.

Tate halted when he spotted her. Those gray-blue eyes met hers, catapulting her back in time to the night she'd watched from the bleachers with the rest of the pep band as he scored a three-pointer at the buzzer and claimed the state championship. While his teammates and cheerleaders swarmed him near half-court, he'd turned and looked for her. The grin he'd flashed had sealed the deal. She'd fallen in love with her best friend.

The little girl collided with Tate's legs. She stumbled, dropped her suitcase and crashed into her brother. He fell on all fours in a mud puddle and burst into tears.

"Oh, no." Eliana slung her tote bag over her shoulder and rushed to help.

"You're okay." Tate set his luggage aside and hauled the little boy to his feet. "We'll get you some dry pants once we're inside."

"Hunter, you're such a crybaby." The girl righted the smaller suitcases and shoved her hair out of her eyes with an exasperated sigh.

"Willow, kind words, please." Tate lifted the boy into his arms and pressed a kiss to his forehead. The gesture didn't soften the child's crying, but it poked a hole in the protective barrier Eliana had erected around her heart.

Be strong.

"Anything I can do to help?" The wailing child plucked at all her heartstrings. Regardless of how much Tate's rejection still stung, she couldn't turn away from an injured little kid.

"Eliana." His Adam's apple bobbed as he swallowed. "Hey. It's good to see you."

Is it? She arched an eyebrow. "Would you like to come inside the café? I have a first aid kit and fresh chocolate chip cookies."

The boy lifted his head off Tate's shoulder. "Cookies?"

"May I have some, please?" The little girl leaned her adorable self against Tate's legs. "I love cookies."

Tate's masculine brow formed a line. "That's nice of you to offer, but I don't want to intrude. My mom should be here any minute to let us into the apartment."

"You're staying here?"

Why did she have to sound so surprised?

He shifted the boy in his arms. "For now. By the way, these are my children, Willow and Hunter."

For now. That sounded temporary. She could handle temporary. Maybe. Unless his wife showed up.

"Nice to meet you, Hunter and Willow. My name is Eliana. I'm a…friend of your dad's."

Something undecipherable flickered across Tate's handsome features then disappeared.

"Your mom left on a flight this morning to help Dr. Rasmussen see patients out in Little Creek Cove. She's probably running late. Why don't you come inside the café?"

Tate settled Hunter on his feet and examined the scrapes on the boy's palms.

Eliana took advantage of the opportunity to study Tate. He looked good. Really good. Especially holding a distraught child. He wore his coffee-brown hair short on the sides and back but longer on top. The boyish face from her memories had matured. A five o'clock shadow marched along his angular jawline, and his broad shoulders filled out his expensive orange Gore-Tex jacket.

His eyes found hers again, and she willed her pulse not to accelerate. She suspected that gaze still held the power to undo her.

"We'd like to accept your kind offer."

"Follow me." She turned and led the way to the café's entrance, her obstinate pulse already speeding at full throttle.

Inside, Eliana smiled politely at Skye, the college student she'd hired to work part-time. "Change of plans. An old friend showed up. I'll make the bank deposit later."

"Sounds good." Skye's curious gaze slid toward Tate and the twins coming in behind her. A handful of customers sat at the tables in the dining room. The café served mostly pie and coffee at this point in the afternoon. Skye circulated with the coffee carafe, offering refills and answering questions about activities on the island.

Willow skipped toward the counter and climbed up on the leather stool where her grandfather had sat hours earlier.

"Is this your restaurant?" she asked, already spinning her stool in a circle.

Eliana stifled a smile at the way the little girl turned all her *r*'s to *w*'s. So cute. "Your grandparents own it. I'm the manager."

Willow's little eyebrows scrunched together.

"Yeah, it's complicated," Eliana said, offering a silent prayer that the answer would satisfy the girl's curiosity.

"I'm going to help Hunter change clothes." Tate set their suitcases down beside an empty booth and unzipped one of the smaller ones. "Is it okay if Willow stays with you?"

"Absolutely." Eliana retrieved the small first aid kit from the shelf under the register then brought it to him. "Bathrooms are at the end…"

She trailed off. He knew exactly where the bathrooms were. His family owned the place. He'd spent plenty of time here over the years.

"Thanks." He tucked clothes under his arm, grabbed Hunter's hand and took the plastic box from Eliana. She allowed her eyes to linger on his strong, capable hands. "Be right back."

Willow stopped spinning and hopped off the stool. "Can we have cookies now?"

"First, we need to go on a secret mission." Eliana angled her head toward the kitchen. "I think you're the perfect woman for the job."

Willow's blue eyes grew wider. "Secret mission?"

Eliana paused beside Willow's stool and held out her hand. "We need to find the milk. I can't possibly serve cookies without glasses of cold milk."

Willow twined her little fingers with Eliana's, sending a bolt of surprise zinging through her. This was Tate's little girl. Holding her hand. How had this happened? She wouldn't think about it. Couldn't think about it. Hunter had fallen practically right in front of her. She couldn't leave them all standing outside in the rain, locked out of their apartment, when the café was right here. With fresh chocolate chip cookies to distract them. It was a favor. Nothing more. Sure, Tate had crushed her when he'd left. But she'd take the high road here. Be the bigger person. She'd never been good at holding a grudge, anyway.

A few minutes later, armed with a half gallon of milk, a platter of cookies and four glasses, Eliana led Willow from the kitchen back to the café.

Willow hummed an unfamiliar tune as she trotted around the counter and scrambled back onto the stool. Eliana barely had the cap twisted off the milk before Willow took the container and started pouring.

"Boy, you are good at this." Eliana smiled. "You must help your mommy in the kitchen a lot."

Willow tucked her tongue in one corner of her mouth while she poured milk into a second glass. "Mommy doesn't cook. She makes her new husband do it. My daddy cooks, though."

"What does Daddy do?" Tate's voice interrupted Eliana's reeling thoughts. Willow and Hunter's mom had a new husband. Which meant...

"You cook for us." Willow beamed at her father. "Look, we have cookies."

Tate's amiable smile and the adorable child in his arms

sent Eliana's imagination on a wild trek through the wilderness of a future she'd never thought possible.

This sensational piece of breaking news raced through her head faster than the headlines scrolling on a cable television channel.

Not that it mattered. None of her business. Her feelings for Tate had been an innocent childhood crush. An infatuation his family had never approved of. He'd chosen loyalty to his parents when he started a family, started a life, with Jade.

Although she'd be lying if the notion that Jade and he were no longer together didn't give her the tiniest bit of satisfaction.

"This place looks great, El."

El. Tate hadn't called her that in years. Her heart pranced with delight, like a sled dog eager to sprint, but she quickly pulled back the reins. *Whoa, girl.*

"I could make it look even better if your family would accept my offer." She pinned him with a meaningful gaze. "Those trees between the café and the office need to go, then I'd have room to bump out this wall and expand the dining area. A fireplace and booths with banquette seating would be amazing."

"Wow, I can see you've given this a lot of thought." Tate smiled. "I think it's great that you care so much about what happens with the café."

"Yeah, well, apparently you're the only one in your family who appreciates my dedication."

Oh, wow. She bit her lip. Tate had been home less than an hour. It was too soon for snarky comments about their families' dispute. She grabbed the spray bottle from under the counter and a roll of paper towels and started squirting down the countertop, moving as far from Tate as possible.

His concerned gaze tracked her every move.

"Eliana—"

She jutted her chin toward the window. "Your dad and brother are here. I've got to get going. Leave the cups. I'll clean up."

Silence hovered between them. Even Willow and Hunter watched them without speaking.

"All right." Tate stood. "C'mon, guys. Grandpa Rex and Uncle Christian are outside. Let's go say hi. Tell Eliana thank you."

"Thank you," they both chimed sweetly in unison.

"You're welcome." Eliana waved to the twins. "It was nice to meet you."

"See you around." Tate herded his children toward their luggage and the café's front door.

The door clicked shut. She blew out a long breath, then scrubbed at a coffee stain on the counter with her paper towel. Making an offer to buy the café had dominated her thoughts for so long, finally filling the headspace once devoted to Tate. Now that he was back and no longer married, she'd have to be extra careful not to allow his presence to breathe life into those feelings she'd tried so hard to extinguish.

She would not lose this place without a fight. Even if Tate's entire family conspired against her. And she had exactly ten days to derail their plans.

Chapter Two

The instant Eliana graciously swooped in and rescued him, Tate had remembered all the reasons why he'd admired and respected her. Treasured their friendship. Even though his mother had made it clear that Eliana lived and worked in Hearts Bay, he hadn't been mentally prepared to see her again.

Eliana was beautiful. Her sleek dark hair pulled into a ponytail had replaced the low-maintenance shoulder-length bob etched in his memory. He'd always thought she was cute in high school, but today her golden-brown eyes framed with dark lashes were stunning. She'd ditched her trademark sweatshirts in favor of a stylish cardigan sweater layered over a T-shirt with leggings and flats. Eliana possessed a quiet strength now, a resilience that wasn't there when they were teenagers. The first aid kit had helped, but it was her infinite patience with Willow that captured his attention.

Now he couldn't stop thinking about her.

He stood at the second-story window in the small apartment over his family's charter fishing business and stared at the harbor. Somewhere down there his father and brother, Christian, were giving Willow and Hunter a tour of their boat. The kids had been hyped up on sugar from their visit to the café and zoomed around the apartment like flies at a picnic. Tate was supposed to be unpacking their things and getting settled. So far he'd ordered pizza and started a load of laundry. The brief reprieve from caring for his kids left ample opportunity for his doubts to come marching in and set up shop.

Sure, it felt great to be home. In Idaho, he'd worked for Jade's family building custom houses. Even after the divorce, her uncle had kept him on the payroll. Thankfully, the guy hadn't felt compelled to pick sides and had graciously given him the summer off. Tate enjoyed building and made a good living. The job allowed him to stay actively involved in the kids' lives, and he wanted to keep building houses. But for now, he'd have to settle for fishing part-time for his family's business and helping Willow and Hunter cope with their mother's absence. Part of him hoped the twins would fall in love with Alaska and beg him to come back every summer.

His gaze wandered to the roof of the café, peeking through the limbs and branches of the stately spruce trees dividing their land. The conversation with Eliana about her plans for buying his family's property had surprised him. She'd obviously devoted a lot of time and energy to the café. His family's business likely flourished because of her tireless efforts. What had she meant when she said that no one else appreciated her dedication? Was she bitter that his parents wouldn't sell? Mostly their interaction irritated him because her words had spotlighted one of his biggest shortcomings—his selfishness.

He'd put himself first when he left Hearts Bay behind. Let his childhood friendships fade and left his brother and parents to run the family's businesses. Then he'd married Jade and started working for her family instead. There wasn't anything he could say or do to justify his behavior, other than admit he'd succumbed to pressure from his family to never date a Madden. His parents hadn't criticized his decision to stay in Idaho, but part him felt guilty. Sadly, he'd made a series of poor choices resulting in a marriage that shouldn't have happened. And now that he'd come home, the realization that his and Eliana's families were locked in a stalemate over waterfront property made him want to jump on the next flight out.

He sighed, then scrubbed his hand over his face. How could his father still be so stubborn? He'd heard the story countless times at family gatherings, like a tall tale that only expanded with each retelling. Tate suspected Eliana's grandparents and his grandparents hadn't fought over the land as bitterly as the Adamses claimed. The details were fuzzy, but the result was clear—Eliana's grandfather had argued the land was his because his family had claimed it as their homestead. Tate's grandfather had insisted he had claimed the waterfront property first, but he'd allow the Maddens to rent a portion. It was a convoluted dispute, and the bitter resentment deepened when Eliana's grandmother married Eliana's grandfather instead of Tate's. Never mind that none of the kids, grandkids and great-grandkids would be around if it had gone differently, but that key detail was always conveniently ignored.

Eliana's grandmother had never said a word about Tate falling in love with Eliana. Whenever he saw her, she'd smiled knowingly and chatted with him. His own grandfather hadn't been shy about sharing his perspective, though. Even gone so far as to help pay for Tate's college education in another state. Far, far away from anyone with the last name Madden.

"Well, Pop, you got your way for a little while. But I have a feeling that things aren't going to go the way you'd hoped forever." Tate shook his head. He'd recognized that spark in Eliana's eyes today. She wasn't going to give up on her dream just because his family refused to cooperate.

"Tate?" His mother burst through the door, a whirlwind of plum-colored scrubs, a forest green jacket and a broad smile.

"Hi, Mom." Tate crossed the room and enveloped her in a hug. "It's good to see you."

Tammy Adams pulled back, her brown eyes scanning his face. "I'm so glad you're here. How was your trip?"

He cringed. "Not good. Willow and Hunter were both so excited on the flight that they couldn't sit still. Then they were seasick for most of the ferry ride."

Her dark eyes darted around the living area. "Where are they?"

"Dad and Christian took them down to check out the boat. Willow, as usual, had about a zillion questions."

Mom smiled, then hung up her jacket on the hook next to his. "I can't wait to see them. It's been too long."

It had. She and Dad had visited Boise a handful of times over the years, but they hadn't seen Willow and Hunter since the previous summer.

"I'm sorry we accidentally locked you out." Mom set her bag on the floor, then slipped out of her sneakers. "We had to quit hiding the key after a former employee stole out of the till last summer. Dr. Rasmussen and I got delayed out in Little Creek Cove, so we were late getting back. Anyway, where did you hang out while you waited?"

He jammed his hands in the back pockets of his jeans. "The café. Eliana fed the kids milk and cookies."

"Oh." Mom's brows disappeared under her bangs. Then she moved past him toward the kitchen. "How'd that go?"

"Fine." Didn't it? "Well, sort of. Until she mentioned she wants to buy us out and take down the trees so she can expand the café."

His mom didn't respond. Only soaped up her hands, then took an excessively long time scrubbing them at the kitchen sink.

"I ordered pizza." He leaned against the counter behind her. "It should be here soon."

"Great." She avoided eye contact as she dried her hands, then opened the refrigerator. "I bought you some groceries so you wouldn't have to go out again tonight. Do your kids like salad?"

"Not really." Tate linked his arms across his chest. "What are you not telling me?"

"Pardon?"

"I can tell you're debating if you should say something. Or not. You're terrible at hiding your feelings, by the way."

She retrieved a bowl from the lower cabinet and set it on the counter beside him.

"Mom, please. Spill it."

"Your dad accepted an offer from a developer. We're supposed to meet with our attorney and sign the paperwork next Friday."

Tate's stomach plummeted. "What developer?"

She ripped open the bag of salad, then dumped it into

the bowl. "A family from Portland wants to put in a hotel and convention center right here."

His laughter echoed through the small kitchen. "You're kidding."

Mom returned to the fridge and pulled out a bag of carrots. "What's funny about a legitimate offer?"

"Orca Island already has a resort, motels, plus bed-and-breakfasts. Who needs a fancy hotel or a convention center?"

"You'd be surprised. Things have changed. People want to get married here in front of the heart-shaped rocks, and there's not a venue large enough for their receptions."

"What's wrong with the resort or community center? Or the basement at the Baptist church?"

"That's cute that you think a modern bride would settle for any of those options."

"I find it hard to believe that the wedding industry has transformed the island's popularity."

Or that a few high-maintenance brides had the power to undermine Eliana's business plan.

"I told you." Mom pulled out a cutting board and a knife to slice the carrots. "Things have changed around here."

Not everything. You guys are still fighting the same old fight. He swallowed back that observation. "What's going to happen to these buildings?"

"That's up to the new owner, but I imagine he'll knock them down."

No. "What about Eliana?"

She studied him, her knife hovering over the cutting board. "Honey, this offer is too good to pass up."

"But it will close the café. What about the employees, who probably have families to feed?"

Mom's mouth tightened in a small line. Her knife deftly sliced the carrot into coins. "Eliana can find a new venue if she wants to open her own café. The other employees will find new jobs, probably at the new hotel."

"Or maybe this developer can find an alternate location for his swanky hotel." Tate's voice rose. Mom's chin lifted. The flash of anger in her brown eyes indicated that he'd crossed some invisible line.

She scraped the carrots into the salad. "I know how much you valued your friendship with Eliana when you were kids, but there's a lot of water under that bridge. Your father and I aren't willing to reject this offer so she can keep her job. We'd like to eventually move out of state, and this offer is a wonderful opportunity to start making our plans a reality."

Unbelievable. How could she be so cavalier about people's livelihood?

Someone knocked on the door. Tate pushed away from the counter. "I'll get it. Hopefully, that's the pizza."

"Tate, I—"

He held up his hand. "Let's continue this conversation when Dad and Christian are here. Not that my opinion holds much weight, but I'm not going to let you ruin something that she's worked so hard to maintain. For you."

"I told them those trees had to go," Eliana whispered.

Early the next morning, she stood in front of the café, hands pressed to her cheeks. Tears blurred her vision. The Sitka spruce, once stately and elegant, had smashed through the café's roof. An angry, gnarled mess of branches, boughs and trunk fragments had cut an alarming swath of destruction right through the heart of the business.

Her whole world.

"Eliana?" Tate jogged toward her, his expression stricken. "I'm—"

"Don't." She sniffed and held out her arm to stop him from getting close to her. "Don't pretend to care. It's too late. I told your parents that those trees had to come down. But did anyone listen? No. Of course not. Because you're all more concerned about selling out and…and… sailing off into the sunset with a boatload of cash."

Whoa. Where did that come from?

Tate's eyes widened. A muscle ticked in his cheek. "That's not fair."

"Easy for you to say. You didn't just lose your job." She turned and stormed away, her throat burning and cheeks damp with another fresh wave of tears.

A fire engine, a police car, the truck from the utility company and some friends with chain saws had assembled in the parking lot in front of the café. The rest of the people gathered were her usual morning customers. The sign in the front window was still flipped to Closed. Sadly, that would be the case for a while. Or maybe forever? If Rex Adams wanted to sell, why not bring in a bulldozer and demolish the entire structure now?

An icy tingle zipped down her spine. He wouldn't. Would he?

"Eliana, wait." Tate's footsteps pounded the asphalt behind her.

"Please go away," she whispered. He was the last person she wanted to see or speak to right now.

She stopped at the edge of a partially caved-in wall—the one she'd hoped to knock down to expand the café's dining area—and whirled to face him. "Your family could have prevented this from happening, so don't pretend to be contrite."

Tate's nostrils flared. He braced his hands on his hips. "I wasn't aware my family had the power to control the wind and the vicious storms that roll in off the Gulf of Alaska. I wonder if my dad knows. If that's the case, I hope he brings fair skies and calm seas from now until his last charter in September."

His biting sarcasm stung. So unlike the Tate she'd once known and loved. Maybe this bitter, caustic version was what she'd have to put up with now. What a shame.

She diverted her attention from his gray T-shirt rippling in the breeze toward the pile of debris at her feet. "I've been dreaming of buying this place for months. I can't decide if your parents don't want the café anymore, or if they just don't want me to have it." Her throat ached with unshed tears. "Our grandparents fought about this land, Tate. Now here we are, staring at a tree that's older than this stupid conflict. When is this all going to end?"

"You have every right to be upset."

The timbre of his voice wound a ribbon of comfort around her heart. *No.* She swept that positive emotion aside before it got comfortable.

Tate huffed out a breath. She pretended not to notice as he swept his fingers through his damp hair.

"Look." He stepped closer and lowered his voice. "I can't change what's already happened and surely can't undo the things that the generations before us have done, but if you'd stop yelling at me for two seconds, I might have a solution. Something that works for both of us."

"I wasn't yelling."

"Um, I'm quite confident the people boarding the ferry heard you."

"Don't be dramatic. I wasn't *that* loud."

The corner of his mouth twitched.

She felt the gazes of curious onlookers, circled up and watching their drama unfold in the parking lot. Their families' conflict might've reached across decades, but somehow folks never seemed to tire of spectating. Plucking a café napkin from the pocket of her cardigan, she dabbed at the moisture on her cheeks. "All right, let's hear your grand plan."

"I've built over thirty houses in Idaho, which means I've learned a few things about construction. Once the insurance claim is filed and they issue a check to cover the cost of repairs, I'd be happy to help rebuild."

"That's sweet of you to offer, but isn't your dad selling the property to a developer? What's the point of repairing a building that's going to be demolished?"

Tate frowned. "Nothing's for sure yet."

"But this tree just made your father's decision to sell that much easier." She plucked her phone from the back pocket of her jeans and brushed past him. "Thanks for the offer, but I'll pass."

"Eliana, please. Hear me out."

She halted her steps. Her name on his lips softened her defenses. Turning back to face him, she braced for the one-two punch his empathetic gaze would no doubt inflict. "This isn't a good idea."

"Why not?"

"Because there's way too much history between us."

Hurt flashed in his eyes. She pressed her palm to her

forehead. This wasn't what she wanted. She really didn't want to hurt him.

Okay, so maybe that wasn't exactly true. She kind of wanted him to hurt. At least a little, because he'd wounded her so deeply when he'd left. It was already going to be a long, hard summer with him living here. She couldn't handle him managing the repairs, too.

"What if I said I needed your help?"

"Help with what?"

"I'll supervise the repairs while you help me out with Willow and Hunter. The woman I had lined up took another job in Anchorage to be closer to her boyfriend. The café is going to be closed for a while. How are you planning to spend your time?"

Her stomach clenched. "I haven't thought that far ahead yet. I'm hoping there's a way your folks can still pay their employees, at least for a couple of weeks."

"That's why you need to consider my suggestion. If you help me with Willow and Hunter, you'll have some extra income."

What I need is for your family to decline that offer. She fought to keep her anger in check. Another snide comment wouldn't help. "I'm not that great with kids, and you have twins."

"What are you talking about? You're amazing with kids."

"Hanging out for a few minutes and serving milk and cookies are not the same as helping them learn the alphabet and doing crafts."

"They don't have to learn anything. It's summer. And they're four. Willow and Hunter need someone to keep them safe, fed and occupied while I'm working."

"That sounds exhausting. Like I said, it's a no for

me." She stepped around him, determined to put space between them. The monster tree had disrupted her life and put the restaurant's staff out of work. She felt vulnerable. Discouraged. This wasn't the time to let her old feelings for Tate cloud her thinking.

"So that went well," Tate grumbled as he strode back to his family's office and the apartment.

"Daddy, Aunt Sarah throwed up." Willow greeted him in the doorway.

"Two times." Hunter squeezed in beside his sister and thrust two fingers in the air. "It's yuck."

Tate had brought the twins downstairs so he could meet with his sister-in-law, Sarah, and get reacquainted with how she scheduled reservations for the fishing charters, processed payments and collected signed waivers. When he'd noticed the tree lying across the café and the parking lot, he'd asked Sarah to keep an eye on Willow and Hunter while he spoke to Eliana about the damage.

"Daddy, what happened?" Hunter ducked under Willow's arm braced against the door frame and stepped barefoot out onto the concrete. "Who knocked down that tree?"

"There was a storm last night, buddy." Tate ruffled Hunter's curls. "You shouldn't be out here without shoes on."

"Didn't you hear the wind?" Willow tossed her head proudly. "My clock is messed up. That means we losted our power."

"We did?" Hunter scrunched his nose, glancing up at Tate to confirm whether his sister was pulling a fast one on him.

"Our electricity was out for a little while, but everything works now. Let's check on Aunt Sarah." He followed the kids inside the office and closed the door.

Sarah emerged from the bathroom, her skin pasty and pale.

Uh-oh. Tate leaned his elbows on the counter dividing the office space from the cozy waiting area. "Are you all right?"

Sarah shook her head and sank into the chair behind the desk tucked in the corner.

"She needs crackers." Willow clung to the edge of the counter and tried to walk up the cabinet base like a monkey.

"And ginger ale." Hunter flopped on the bench against the wall and retrieved his favorite stuffed animal, a faded brown puppy dog. "Mommy gives us ginger ale when our tummies are sad."

Sarah tipped her head back against the chair. "I'm not that kind of sick."

"But you look sick," Hunter said.

"Hunter." Tate shot him a warning glance. "Be nice. And Willow, don't climb on stuff."

Willow huffed out her breath then let go of the counter, crossed to the bench and flopped down beside her brother.

Sarah's worried gaze found Tate's. "We weren't quite ready to tell anyone yet. Christian wanted to wait until I saw the doctor just to be sure, but I'm positive this morning sickness means I'm pregnant."

"Wow, did you hear that?" Tate grinned at his children. "Aunt Sarah has a baby growing in her tummy."

Willow's eyes rounded, and she shot to her feet and raced around the counter. "Can I see?"

"Congratulations," Tate said. "That's awesome!"

"Thanks." Sarah smiled weakly and pulled Willow onto her lap. "This isn't exactly good news for you, though."

Tate frowned. "What do you mean?"

"I'm going to need your help if I'm throwing up every ten minutes. I can't work in here or keep an eye on Willow and Hunter. Have you found anyone to watch your kids yet?"

Tate averted his gaze and peeked through the window. Eliana stood in the middle of a pile of debris, her phone pressed to her ear. If only she'd said yes.

"I'm guessing your grand plan got shot down?" Sarah asked.

Willow gasped. "Who got shot?"

Sarah winced. "Sorry, poor choice of words."

"No one got shot, sweet pea. It's an expression. I'm trying to figure out who's going to stay with you while I'm fishing." Tate palmed the back of his neck. He'd stayed up late scouring local social media sites for a lead on half-day camps or college-age students home for the summer who might want to nanny. And now Sarah looked miserable, which meant he was back to square one.

"What about Grandma and Aunt Sarah?" Willow played with a strand of Sarah's long blond hair. "They can watch us."

"I wish I could, pumpkin." Sarah kissed the top of Willow's head. "I'm not feeling well."

"Grandma works at the clinic with Dr. Rasmussen three days a week." Tate pulled his phone from his pocket. A new text message from Eliana's sister Tess lit up the screen.

I heard there are two spots available in half-day camp at the community center. 9am to noon, Monday through Friday, starting next week. Are you interested?

Thank You, Lord.

Yes, please. How do I sign up?

He sent the text, then put his phone down on the counter. Willow turned her best puppy dog eyes his way. Oh, boy. He mentally fortified his shields.

"We could go fishing with you." She added a sweet smile. "Me and Hunter are good helpers."

Tate tried not to laugh. Sarah covered her mouth with her hand to silence her chuckle. His father and brother would come unglued if they heard four-year-old twins were their deckhands for the rest of the summer. The first time Hunter saw someone gaff their catch, he'd melt into a puddle of tears.

"I'm sure Grandpa Rex will take you fishing sometime. Right now he has customers scheduled, and he needs my help. It wouldn't be fair for me to bring you along with us. Don't worry, I'll find someone safe to stay with you."

Willow pooched out her lower lip. "I don't want you to go."

"Me, either," Hunter whined. "Grandpa already has Uncle Christian to help."

Tate's chest tightened. The last thing he wanted was to cause his kids more pain. They already had to spend the summer without their mother.

"Eliana might change her mind," Sarah said. "Give

her time. She's probably in shock, and her whole world's been turned upside down by that tree."

"My suggestion that we work together to solve each other's problems didn't help, either." Tate sank down on the bench beside Hunter. Man, he missed the days when hanging out with Eliana was effortless. Evenings. Weekends. Parties after basketball games. They had been the best of friends.

Now she acted like she couldn't stand the sight of him. Not that he could blame her, given he'd left the island and chosen to marry Jade. If only he could find his way back to the relationship with Eliana he'd once had. Before he'd so carelessly trampled all over it.

Hunter climbed up in his lap. "I'm hungry."

"We just had breakfast." Tate checked the clock on the wall. It was only eight thirty. "Let me talk to Aunt Sarah for a few minutes, then we'll get a snack."

Hunter nodded, then rested his head against Tate's shoulder. Poor kid. He was probably exhausted.

"Has Christian talked to you about his job interview?" Sarah asked.

"No," Tate said. "We haven't had much time to catch up yet."

"He's looking for something more permanent with better health insurance, especially now that your parents want to sell. If he gets the job with the Department of Transportation, you'll need to be the deckhand."

Oh, boy. Now he definitely needed reliable childcare.

The office door opened, and Eliana stepped inside.

"Can I speak to you, please?" Her gaze slid to Hunter. "Privately?"

"I'm okay if you want to step outside," Sarah offered. "Willow and Hunter can help me restock brochures."

"Thank you."

Tate lifted Hunter off his lap, but Hunter looped his arms around Tate's neck and squeezed. "I want to stay with you."

Sarah motioned for Willow and Hunter to move closer. "C'mon, kiddos. Help me open this box of brochures."

Willow twirled in a circle beside Sarah's chair. "What's a brochure?"

"Look." Sarah pulled scissors from her desk drawer. "I'll show you."

Tate hugged Hunter, then gently set him on his feet. "Go with Aunt Sarah. I'll be back in a few minutes."

Once Sarah and the kids were occupied, Tate followed Eliana outside.

When she faced him, he faked an indifferent expression and stuffed his clammy palms in the back pockets of his jeans. Had she discovered more damage from the tree?

She drew her red cardigan sweater tighter around her petite frame. "I'll watch Willow and Hunter on one condition."

His breath caught in his chest. "Name it."

"You have until next Friday to convince your family not to sell the property. If your parents sign the papers, then you'll have to find a new babysitter."

He barked out a laugh. "Anything else?"

She shrugged, then turned to leave. "Just thought I'd offer. Hope you find someone to watch your twins."

No! Panic welled. Since the woman he'd hired had changed her plans, his list of reliable babysitters was nonexistent. Other than the day camp, which he still hadn't completely nailed down, he was out of options.

"Wait."

One hand on the door, Eliana glanced back over her shoulder. Those golden-brown eyes glinted with fierce determination. He couldn't mess this up.

"The truth is, I need your help. Willow and Hunter need your help. I don't know if I can convince Mom and Dad to change their minds, but I'll try my best. If you'd be willing to pick the twins up from camp at noon and keep them until I finish working here in the office or else come back from a charter, I'd appreciate it."

She quirked her lips to one side. "Are you sure you can afford me?"

"I don't have the luxury of being a cheapskate."

His attempt at a joke fell miserably flat. She frowned and pulled out her phone.

"Fifteen dollars an hour sounds reasonable." Her fingers flew over her screen. "Seven hours a day, five days a week, that's five hundred and twenty-five dollars a week."

He gulped. More expensive than a summer's worth of daycare in Boise, which was what he would've done had they stayed in Idaho. Still, with the addition of the camp costs, he'd have to dip into his savings.

"Tate?" She studied him. "Do we have a deal?"

"Can you start Monday?"

"What time?"

"Their camp is over at noon. Can you pick them up and stay until I get home around six?"

She nodded.

"Perfect." The sinking feeling in his gut began to lift. "Thank you."

Tucking her phone back in her pocket, she gave him a tight smile. "The clock's ticking. You have a little over a week to convince your family to reject that offer."

Her words squelched his short-lived relief over solving his childcare dilemma. "Right."

He blew out a long breath and went back inside the office. His chances of convincing his parents to change their minds were slim to none. But that wouldn't stop him from trying, because he was determined to prove to Eliana that he was worthy of her trust.

Chapter Three

Note to self: a strong-willed four-year-old is a force to be reckoned with.

Eliana refused to bend the rules to accommodate Willow's preferences. No matter how adorable the little girl looked with her curls twisted into two bouncy pigtails. "Willow, you have to wear a helmet if you're going to ride a scooter."

"Fine." Willow let her new scooter drop to the ground and crossed her arms over her pale pink T-shirt. "I'll walk."

Her defiant gaze made Eliana want to scream.

Hunter's lower lip trembled. "No, Willow. We have to try our new scooters."

"He's right," Eliana said. "It would be a shame not to ride them, especially on such a beautiful day."

They stood on the sidewalk in front of the café, the June sunshine warming their skin. Tammy Adams had delivered new scooters and helmets while the twins were at their first day of camp. Then she and Eliana had met with the insurance adjuster. The building required substantial repairs from the damage inflicted by the tree, even more than she'd anticipated. Eliana had blinked back more tears at the news. She hadn't missed the victorious smile Tammy had tried to smother behind her hand, though.

"Willow." Hunter glared at his sister. "Come. On."

"Willow, if you can't obey, we're going back inside. You'll lie in your bed and have an hour of quiet time instead of going to the park. Is that what you want?"

Hunter's face crumpled. He went boneless. His scooter tipped over and crashed to the sidewalk. Sinking to the ground, he sobbed loud enough to earn a few curious stares from tourists walking by.

Lord, what have I gotten myself into? Eliana prayed as she pulled out her phone and started a timer. "Willow, you have thirty seconds to put on that helmet or we're going inside."

Eliana showed her the phone screen with the stopwatch running. Willow glanced at it, then looked away.

Less than two hours on the job and she was already locked in a battle of wills with a four-year-old.

Come on, kiddo. Please do the right thing. She did not want to put the scooters away unused and take them both upstairs, but she couldn't back down. Not now. Or it would be a long summer filled with Willow testing her boundaries and trying to seize control of every situation. The little girl's behavior surprised Eliana. She clearly had far more energy and spunk than her cautious, sweet-spirited twin.

Eliana's sister Tess walked toward them with her son, Cameron, riding beside her on his scooter. "Hi, guys." Tess waved. "We thought we'd stop by and say hello."

"Oh, bless you." Eliana flung her arms around her sister's neck. "I'm so glad you're here."

Tess laughed and patted her back. "Somehow I knew you might need backup today."

"You have no idea." Eliana pulled away and turned toward the twins. "Hunter and Willow, this is my sister Tess and her son, Cameron."

"Hi!" Cameron circled around Tess and Eliana on his scooter. He wore an orange helmet accessorized with neon-green rubber spikes.

Hunter stopped crying and swiped at his cheeks with the sleeve of his sweatshirt. His blue eyes tracked Cameron's every move.

"Want to go to the park with us?" Tess asked. "It's right around the corner."

"We'd love to." Eliana slung her backpack over her shoulders. "As soon as Willow agrees to wear her helmet."

"Look at my helmet." Cameron stopped and thumped his knuckles against the hard plastic shell. "Mine has a mohawk."

"Mine has pink sparkles," Willow bragged. "And rainbows and unicorn stickers."

"Watch how fast I can go." Cameron zipped toward the café. He had turned eight recently, so he was taller and weighed more than the twins. But Eliana noted Willow's hardened expression as she watched him go. Eliana nudged Tess in the ribs and pinched her mouth tight to keep from laughing. The little girl did not like to be outdone.

"I can go faster than that," Willow declared.

"Great." Tess smiled. "Put on your helmet and show us."

Willow blew an errant curl out of her eyes and retrieved her helmet from the ground. Then she clipped the buckle under her chin and grabbed her scooter.

"Race you," she yelled, then zipped off, leaving Hunter behind.

"Hey!" Hunter scrambled to his feet. "No fair."

Groaning, Eliana shot Tess a *save me* look.

The fragrance of chopped wood still hung in the air. Tree removal had paused while the workers took their lunch break. Blue tarps covered the building's exposed areas. Tate had gone fishing on a charter with his dad and Christian. She'd already refereed a disagreement over who sat in which car seat when she'd picked them up from camp. During lunch in the apartment upstairs, they'd fought over the color of the cups, nearly spilling water all over the table.

"Wait for me." Hunter hopped on his scooter and hurried after his sister and Cameron.

"I owe you a week's worth of lattes from the coffee shop," Eliana said, falling into step beside her sister as they trailed the kids toward the park.

"Noted." Tess chuckled. "I'll collect at my leisure."

"How did you know I needed help?"

"I meant to text and see if you'd meet us at the park, but Cam wanted to watch some of the fishing boats in the harbor first, so it was easier to walk over. I saw you standing here and figured you were having a bit of a battle."

"What was your first clue? Willow's body language, perhaps?"

"And the helmet on the ground. Crying is also a sign that someone's not happy."

Eliana winced. "Did you hear Hunter crying down at the harbor?"

"Relax." Tess patted her shoulder. "He wasn't that loud."

"I guess I'm extra sensitive." Eliana kept her voice low. "Kids make me nervous, and we're off to a rough start."

"I'm sure you're doing fine," Tess said. "This is a big adjustment for everyone."

"Do you think that's why they're squabbling so much? Still adjusting?"

She and Tess walked together along the sidewalk. Hunter tapped his sneaker on the concrete, his wheels barely rolling. Willow scooted as fast as her little body allowed, desperate to catch Cameron, who was almost to the community park. The play structure, with its paved path circling the perimeter, came into view. Kids' chatter filled the air, and a black dog chased a tennis ball across the green grass.

"Willow's acting out because she doesn't like not having control," Tess said. "Remember, this is a lot for a preschooler to comprehend. They've moved to Alaska without their mom. Nothing is familiar, and now their dad is busy. They have different grandparents and strangers invading, telling them what to do."

"When you put it like that, I feel bad." Eliana shed her backpack and sank down on a bench at the edge of the playground. "Poor things have had a lot thrown at them."

Tess sat beside her and offered an empathetic smile. "Everyone needs lots of grace, including you. You lost your job unexpectedly, and now you've had to pivot. Caring for two young children is an enormous responsibility. This is quite generous, what you're doing for Tate and his kids."

"My options were limited," Eliana said. "A tree landing on a roof can really wreck a girl's summer plans."

"You could have said no."

"I tried that." Eliana craned her neck to see what Hunter and Willow were doing, huddled together under the slide with Cameron. "Tate was persistent."

"Really," Tess teased. "I doubt he had to twist your arm. Since you've been alive, you have held a soft spot in your heart for Tate Adams."

Eliana shot her a playful glare. "Oh, that is not true."

"It's absolutely true." Tess crossed one leg over the other. "That boy could always convince you to do just about anything."

"Plot twist—this time he has to convince his parents to change their plans."

"Tell me more."

"We made a deal. He has to persuade his parents not to sell the property to a real estate developer and to sell it to me instead, otherwise I'm not willing to babysit the twins."

Tess's eyes grew wide. "What about the tree on the roof?"

"Good question." Eliana scrunched her nose. "The insurance adjuster came out today. Tammy says they'll get an estimate on the repairs from a contractor, but I don't believe her. If they plan to sell, why not bulldoze the thing and let the developer do what he wants?"

"I hope they change their mind." Tess sagged against the bench. "I'd hate for you to lose your job at the café, and Hearts Bay doesn't need a luxury hotel or a convention center."

"I agree. Trying not to get my hopes up, though."

"Hopes for the café or hopes about Tate?"

Warmth blossomed on her cheeks. Leave it to Tess to reroute the conversation back to romance. "I'm not getting involved with Tate. He probably won't stick around. His ex-wife will want the twins to move back to Idaho."

"Will she, though?"

"Have you heard differently?"

Tess twisted her dark hair into a ponytail and secured it with an elastic she'd pulled from her wrist. "I haven't heard much. Only that Jade remarried and Tate brought the kids here so she could focus on her new husband."

"Maybe that's why Willow's being so feisty." Eliana cupped her hands to her mouth. "Willow, be careful."

The little girl had climbed to the top of the tallest slide. Hunter and Cameron were still examining a treasure they'd discovered on the ground.

"It doesn't matter to me what Jade does. I've never met the woman, but there's no way I'm going to let myself get attached to Tate."

Or his children.

"Yeah, that's what I said, too." Tess slung her arm around Eliana's shoulders. "Now I'm married to the guy who broke my heart, and we're a family of three."

"I can't do it." Eliana shook her head. "It's too complicated."

"Hey, I get it. When Asher moved back, I was dead set against giving him a second chance."

"While you helped Cameron learn to read, you and Asher fell madly in love all over again, and now you're living the dream," Eliana teased, pressing the back of her hand to her forehead and pretending to swoon.

"Make fun of me all you want, but it can happen to you, too."

"No, it can't. Hunter and Willow are not mine. You

and Asher are both Cameron's parents. There's a big difference."

"It feels like a big difference right now," Tess said. "It's funny how details like that become less important."

"I'm not changing my mind." Eliana straightened and linked her arms across her chest, determined to prove her sister wrong. "Tate and I were teenagers who cared about each other as friends. Yes, I wanted something more, but he chose Jade, and now it's too late."

Tess's expression grew serious. "It's never too late."

Eliana clamped her mouth tight to keep from arguing. Tess might've reunited with her childhood sweetheart, but that didn't mean Eliana and Tate could make a fresh start. Not with this fight over the land still festering, and not with her heart still aching from his poor choices. She wouldn't allow herself to love Tate Adams again.

The charter boat glided into the harbor, its coolers filled with fresh salmon and four satisfied customers smiling from the back deck.

Tate stood at the bow, the cool breeze nipping at his cheeks. Dad guided the boat from his captain's chair inside the cabin. Christian stood with their customers, offering advice about where they should eat for dinner and taking one last picture as they posed for the camera.

Scanning the dock, Tate searched for Eliana and the kids. He'd texted her a few minutes ago and invited her to meet them so Willow and Hunter could see the cooler full of salmon. Well, Willow would enjoy it. Hunter would probably cringe and run the other way. He didn't like anything slimy or smelly, much to Grandpa Rex's dismay.

Eliana hadn't responded yet. He didn't want to bother her, since today was her first day taking care of his kids.

Keeping four-year-old twins safe, fed and entertained was a big job, especially during the late-afternoon hours, when tempers flared and patience ran low. Sometimes he could barely stay one step ahead of meeting the twins' needs, much less answer a text.

He reached for his phone to check for a new message when he spotted her waiting. His pulse sped. She held Willow and Hunter by the hand and leaned down as they pointed and chattered and probably quizzed her relentlessly.

Man, she was gorgeous with her long hair streaming over her red T-shirt. Her blue jeans flared at the bottom over white sneakers, and she'd tied her camouflage-print jacket around her waist. Her sunglasses sat on top of her head, serving as a headband. As the boat moved closer, he realized Willow, Hunter and Eliana all sported temporary tattoos on their cheeks.

Eliana looked tired but happy. Hunter smothered a yawn, and Willow shoved her curls out of her eyes. What had happened to her pigtails that he'd styled for her this morning? She grinned and waved. Her messy hair didn't seem to be an issue.

The knot that had lodged behind his sternum and stayed there all day loosened as he soaked in their smiles. Maybe they'd had a good time together. Maybe he'd worried for nothing.

Cottony white clouds dotted the baby blue sky overhead as Rex guided their boat into the designated slip in the harbor. The sun inched toward Mount Larsen, and the breeze carried the familiar aromas of fish and salt water. Every single muscle in his body ached after spending more than eight hours at sea. But the fatigue and lingering soreness he'd likely deal with tomorrow were all worth it. He hadn't realized how much he needed time on the water, fishing with his dad and Christian. The outing had soothed his weary soul.

"Daddy, Daddy!" Willow and Hunter bounced up and down on the dock. He waved, smiling as Eliana cupped her hands on their shoulders and steadied them.

He liked the way she looked standing there between his children. She might have grudgingly agreed to take this job, but he secretly hoped Willow and Hunter would soften the rough spots in her heart. The wounds he had carved there when he had left her behind.

"Son, grab that line and get Eliana to tie us off, would you?" Dad's deep voice interrupted his thoughts.

"Yep." Tate leaned down and picked up the line, coiling the rope in his hands. "Do you mind tying us off?" he called to Eliana.

"No problem. Step back, please." She gently guided Willow and Hunter behind her.

"Can I help?" Hunter pulled on Eliana's arm.

"No, I want to." Willow stepped in front of him. "You helped with snacks."

Tate caught the irritation pinching Eliana's features as she snagged the line he tossed her. Maybe things hadn't gone as well as he'd hoped. The boat rocked, and Tate shifted his weight to maintain his balance.

"Here, watch." Eliana patiently guided the line through the cleat on the dock, then showed the twins how to secure the boat by twisting the rope into a figure eight.

"There." She straightened and patted them both on the head. "Good teamwork."

"Why don't you go on?" Christian scooted past Tate and hopped onto the dock. "I'll help clean up."

Tate hesitated. "Are you sure? What about Sarah?"

"Her mom came to town last night. They're hanging out and watching a movie. Sarah will be fine." Christian angled his head in Eliana's direction. "Go on. I'm sure it's been a long day."

"Thanks. Next time I'll stay after and you can go home."

Christian nodded. "Sounds like a plan."

Tate said goodbye to their customers, retrieved his duffel bag full of extra clothes and rain gear, then turned to his father. "Thanks for letting me tag along, Dad."

"Sure thing." Rex smiled. "You're a great deckhand."

Well, how about that. He'd even lived up to his father's impossibly high expectations. Slinging his duffel bag over his shoulder, Tate stepped off the boat and onto the dock. Willow and Hunter flung themselves at him, each clinging to one of his legs.

Eliana stepped back, her expression unreadable.

He gently loosened their grip on his filthy jeans. "Hey, kiddos. Did you have fun today?"

"Yes," Hunter said, his eyes gleaming as he smiled up at Tate.

"No." Willow hung her head.

Uh-oh. He'd suspected Willow might give Eliana a hard time.

Eliana cleared her throat. Tate met her gaze. She shook her head ever so slightly. So perhaps there was more to the story.

"Tell me about the fun part, Hunter." Maybe if he received the good news first, Willow's complaints would be more palatable.

"We played tag with Cameron at the park, and Grandma gave us new scooters with helmets."

"That I don't like," Willow added. "Helmets are stupid."

Evidently Willow had decided rules were not for her. "Willow, there's no need for that kind of sassy talk. Helmets are important. They keep you safe." He'd have to speak with her about her attitude and respecting authority. When had his little girl morphed into a defiant tweenager?

Eliana led the way along the dock toward the ramp connecting the harbor to the parking lot. Tate sensed by her silence, hunched shoulders and long strides, she was biting back a snarky comment or two.

"Who is Cameron?" he asked, bringing up the rear.

Eliana paused at the bottom of the ramp and glanced over her shoulder. "My sister Tess and her husband, Asher, have an eight-year-old son named Cameron. They went with us to the park today."

Right. His mom had mentioned Tess had married Asher Hale. Good guy.

Hunter paused to peer at something floating in the water. "We had yummy snacks."

"But we had to take a nap," Willow said. "Mommy never makes me take a nap."

Tate bristled. Jade's loosey-goosey parenting style had followed them all the way to Alaska. Bummer.

"Based on your attitude, I'd say you might need a longer nap tomorrow." Tate reached for the twins' hands as they climbed the steep ramp. "What do you think, Eliana?"

She reached the parking lot first, then kept walking.

The knot wedged behind his sternum again. Something was wrong.

"Where's she going?" Hunter rubbed his eyes with his fist. "I'm sleepy. Who is putting us to bed?"

"I am." Tate led the kids toward their apartment down the street. "We need to eat dinner first."

"Can I take a bath?" Willow asked. "Grandma said she bought us bubble bath and shampoo."

"We'll see," Tate mumbled, staring at Eliana's retreating back as she wove through a group of people strolling along the waterfront.

"Daddy, will you carry me?" Hunter slowed his steps. "My legs are tired."

Tamping down a groan, Tate swung Hunter into his arms, adjusted his duffel bag, then trudged down the sidewalk. Willow skipped along beside them, singing a song from one of her favorite movies.

They crossed the street where his mother stood outside the office. She waved and greeted them. "I brought dinner over. Thought you might appreciate a hot meal after a long day on the water."

"Yes, please." Tate set Hunter on the ground. "Could you take the kids inside while I speak to Eliana?"

Mom's gaze skittered toward Eliana, who was already halfway to her car parked in a space near the café's front door. "Sure."

"Thanks." He leaned down and gave Willow his most piercing stare. "Willow, I want you to go inside and do exactly as your grandmother says. Do you understand?"

Her eyes widened, then she nodded. "Yes."

"Good." He straightened and patted Hunter's shoulder. "Go with Grandma. I'll be right in."

"Do you guys like spaghetti?" his mother asked, unlocking the office door and stepping inside. Hunter and

Willow trailed after her, freely sharing all their thoughts and opinions about spaghetti.

Tate jogged after Eliana. "Hang on a sec."

She hesitated, one hand on her open car door. Pebbles crunched under his shoes as he rounded the back bumper.

Her eyes glistened with unshed tears.

Oh, no. "What happened?"

"I—I don't think I can do this. I mean, I know we had a deal, but there's two of them, and they're constantly fighting. I've never refereed so many arguments in one day."

"Eliana, it's okay. This is normal."

She huffed out a breath and flung her hand in the air. "Look at me, I'm having a meltdown over two high-maintenance preschoolers. This is ridiculous."

"I'm so sorry." He gently clasped her arm. "What can I do?"

She trapped her lower lip behind her teeth. "Find another babysitter."

"What about our agreement?"

She looked away. "It was a silly idea to begin with. Your parents will never change their minds."

His arms ached to pull her into an embrace. But he couldn't. Because he'd only been back in town less than a week. They were barely friends. Acquaintances, really. He forced himself to let go and step back. "I'm sorry that my children are so difficult. But please, please don't give up after the first day."

She gave him the side eye. "You need to have a long talk with Willow. Her attitude is lousy."

"I know. Again, I'm sorry. I'll talk to her. Promise me you'll come back."

Finally, she nodded. "All right. I'll come back tomorrow, and the rest of the week. Friday's not far away, right? I can handle anything—including Willow's attitude—for four days."

"I'm not sure how to respond to that." He pushed his fingers through his hair. "Thank you, I think?"

"See you in the morning." She slid behind the wheel and slammed the door.

As she drove away, he couldn't ignore the feeling settling in his gut. What if she was right? What if he couldn't convince his folks to change their minds?

Chapter Four

U ndone by a four-year-old. How embarrassing.

Eliana sat in the parking lot in front of the café. Workers had cleaned up the tree and hauled the wood away. Only remnants of sawdust on the asphalt and a huge blue tarp stretched across the roof and down the outside wall hinted at the catastrophe. How had she let Willow get under her skin so easily yesterday? She stared at the dark windows. What she wouldn't give for an early shift and a dining room full of hungry customers instead of another day with a petulant child.

Since she couldn't work at the café, she'd planned to attend water aerobics class with Tess at the pool. Then Tate's early-morning text greeted her when she woke up. He'd asked her to stop by because the twins wanted to apologize. How could she possibly refuse?

Lord, please help. I don't think I can do this, but I'm also not a quitter. Grant me an abundance of patience. Amen.

She climbed out of the car, shouldered her backpack and slammed the door.

"Wait." Tate's deep voice cut through the morning

stillness. He hurried toward her, carrying disposable cups from the coffee shop in a cardboard tray.

She met him in front of her car. "What's going on? Where are your kids?"

"They're upstairs with my mom." He held out his hand. "May I take your bag?"

Frowning at the impish gleam in his eyes, she clutched the backpack strap tighter. "Why?"

The corners of his mouth twitched. "I'm trying to be polite. Yesterday was rough. The kids and I have a surprise. Would you like to come upstairs and see?"

Nope. Her feet remained firmly rooted to the concrete. "What kind of a surprise? Your text said they wanted to apologize?"

"Wow, so many questions. You don't trust me?"

She couldn't stop the sharp laugh from bubbling up. "Seriously?"

Pain flickered across his recently shaved face. "I deserve that," he said quietly. "Eliana, I'm sorry. We have a lot we need to talk about."

Please, please not now. She held up her palm. "Why aren't you fishing? I thought your dad's charters left super early?"

His eyes held hers. "I'm staying in town today. Christian can handle this one. There are people here who need my attention."

She commanded her stupid pulse to slow. "What does that mean?"

"I'll show you." Tate reached for her bag again, and this time she handed it over.

Doubt clung to her like a soggy blanket as she followed him up the stairs. The pleasing aroma of his aftershave wafted toward her, and she tried not to think about how much she liked that spicy scent.

At the top of the stairs, she scraped her ballet flats against the welcome mat, then followed Tate inside the apartment.

He set her backpack on the floor against the wall and offered to take her coat.

"Thank you." She shrugged out of the blue anorak and passed it to him, careful to avoid letting her fingers brush against his. He hung her coat on a hook next to Willow's and Hunter's, then angled his head toward the kitchen. "The fun is this way."

Uncertainty prickled her scalp. She'd hit rock bottom in her babysitting misadventures. Fun seemed a long way off. The aroma of bacon sizzling in a pan overruled her hesitation and pulled her toward the kitchen anyway.

Willow and Hunter were balanced on stools at the counter wearing aprons that were far too big for them. Hunter impatiently nudged the brim of a baseball cap sporting the café's logo out of his eyes, then went back to stirring batter in a mixing bowl.

Eliana let her gaze slide to Willow on the stool beside him. Her boat-shaped hat, handmade from paper, tilted precariously between her pigtails.

"Good morning." Tammy stood at the stove, supervising the bacon's progress. She offered a polite smile. "Hope you brought your appetite."

"Good morning." Eliana rubbed her palms against her upper arms. Was the kitchen smaller than she'd remembered? It felt crowded with three adults and the twins filling the cozy space. Maybe she was just anxious. She hadn't planned on sharing a meal or interacting with Tammy this morning. "It smells delicious."

"Willow and Hunter." Tate's voice carried a firm tone. "Remember what we practiced?"

The kids abandoned their utensils, slid off the stools and moved toward Eliana. Her chest tightened. She instinctively took a step back, nearly colliding with Tate.

He handed them each a piece of paper.

Willow tried to make her brother go first, but he hung back, his eyes downcast.

"Go ahead, Willow," Tate prompted.

"I'm sorry about my behavior," Willow whispered. "This is for you."

The regret in her big blue eyes twisted Eliana's insides. Had she expected too much from a preschooler? She accepted the piece of paper with a crayon drawing of a rainbow arching over a boat in the water. "Thank you, Willow. This is beautiful."

Willow readjusted her paper hat on her head. "It's a rainbow above my grandpa's boat."

"Yes, I see that. Well done." Eliana sneaked a glance at Tate. He studied her, as if gauging her reaction.

"Good job, pumpkin," Tate said. "Please let Hunter have a turn."

The little boy crept forward, his eyes already glistening with tears. Eliana ached to pull him into a hug. What a precious child.

"I'm sorry and I'll try my bestest to listen. I made this for you." He held out a picture with trembling hands. "I hope you like it."

Oh, these sweet children. Why had she been so upset with them? She took Hunter's picture of a stick figure fishing on a dock with birds soaring in the blue sky in one hand and motioned for them to come closer with the other. "Thank you for the beautiful pictures. Apologies accepted."

She enveloped them both in a hug and met Tate's eyes over the children's heads. The connection that zinged between them made it impossible to look away. Making her insides melt like a pool of gooey caramel on top of an ice cream sundae had always been Tate's forte.

"Breakfast is almost ready," Tammy announced. "Willow and Hunter, how's that pancake batter coming along?"

Eliana averted her gaze. Leave it to Tammy to ruin a tender moment. She released the kids and straightened. "Your artwork is wonderful. Thank you. Let's have some fun together today." It had been a long time since anyone had given her anything handmade. The kids who came to the diner preferred to keep the coloring pages that came on the back of their menus.

"We made the table nice for you." Hunter pointed toward the retro dining table in the corner. The surface was covered with a white tablecloth. A vase of freshly picked daisies sat in the middle. Paper napkins with a daisy pattern and silverware marked each of the place settings.

"Sit down," Willow said. "I mean, please sit down."

Eliana bit back a smile and crossed to the red vinyl chair closest to the window. She set the kids' drawings on the empty chair beside her.

"What would you like to drink?" Willow asked.

"May I please have coffee and a glass of water?"

Willow nodded. "Coming right up. Daddy, coffee and water, please."

Tate smiled and brought Eliana one of the drinks he'd carried in on the tray. "Annie at the Trading Post said this was your favorite."

"Wow, thank you." She took the cup, eyeing the flavor scribbled on the side in black marker. He'd gone out of his way to buy her favorite beverage. How thoughtful.

It was easy to forget yesterday's struggles when two adorable children and their handsome father offered to fix breakfast. She waited patiently at the table, watching the controlled chaos unfold before her, and tried not to look out the window at the ruined café. Tate's efforts and the kids' apologies were sweet and all, but nothing could unravel their grandparents' plans to keep her from buying him out.

Eliana was a natural with his kids. Her humble attitude and gracious acceptance of their apologies warmed him from the inside out.

Tate leaned against the kitchen counter, savoring his cup of coffee. His mother stood at the sink, washing the last of the pans she'd used to make breakfast. Things had been a little tense between her and Eliana. Evidently not every problem could be solved with pancakes and bacon.

Sarah had opened the office downstairs, insisting that her new medication kept her morning sickness under control, so Mom had grudgingly agreed to spend part of her day off from the medical clinic helping him out. He'd had to grovel, though. She cleared her throat and shot him another pointed glance.

He stifled a smile and drained the last of his coffee. Mom had never been shy about expressing her opinion. But he wasn't going to let her disapproval derail his plans. He had to prove to Eliana that he believed her dreams for owning the café mattered.

Even if his parents didn't.

He tossed his empty cup in the garbage. "Mom, you're going to take the kids to camp, right?"

She dried the skillet and put it back in the cabinet beside the stove without looking at him. "What time do they need to be there?"

Tate glanced at the clock on the microwave. "You'll need to leave in the next few minutes if you're going to get them there by nine."

She straightened and faced him, frowning. "And what are you planning to do while I'm gone?"

"Mom." He lowered his voice and leaned closer. "We talked about this. Sarah feels well enough to work in the office, and you said you were off today so you'd help me out."

"So you can spend more time alone with her."

Her disapproval steamrolled him, flattening his optimistic attitude. Maybe getting her involved in his mission was a mistake. Willow and Hunter kept up a constant stream of chatter, both vying for Eliana's attention. Her familiar laughter bubbled up, reminding him of why he was doing this. Her goals and dreams were important. How she felt about him and his family mattered. Probably more than it should. Since she'd agreed to look after his high-maintenance children, the least he could do was get his parents to reconsider her proposal. And with Friday looming, he didn't have much time to change their minds.

"I don't understand why you care so much," Mom whispered, drying her hands on a dish towel. "You're basically asking us to change our retirement plans to make Eliana happy."

Maybe. He winced then looked toward the table again. Seeing Eliana smile and laugh with his kids, forgiving yesterday's mistakes so easily, made him wonder if she might forgive him, too. Then again, his mother had a point. He was asking his family to consider Eliana's dreams above their own. But what was so wrong with that?

Mom stepped around him. "Willow and Hunter, I'm taking you to camp today. Go put on your shoes and coats, please."

"What about Eliana?" Hunter plucked the last slice of bacon from his plate. "I thought she was watching us today?"

"Eliana will pick you up from camp." Tate moved toward the table with a wet cloth to wipe the twins' sticky hands. "Grandma is leaving, and she's offered to drop you off."

"Thank you for breakfast." Eliana cradled her coffee cup in both hands. "Everything was delicious."

"You're welcome," Tammy said without smiling. She motioned for Willow and Hunter to hurry. "Let's go, kiddos. Time for camp."

The kids scrambled out of Tate's reach. He'd done a passable job of cleaning them up, but he wasn't confident they were completely syrup-free. He cleared the last of the breakfast dishes from the table. "Can I get you anything else?"

Eliana's dark eyes tracked him. "Why are you doing this?"

He hesitated, his hands full of Willow's and Hunter's plates. "Excuse me?"

"I know you wanted the kids to apologize, and don't get me wrong, breakfast was lovely, but what's going on?"

He set the dirty dishes onto the counter, checked to make sure his mother was occupied with getting the twins out the door, then sat down across from Eliana. "It's important to me that you understand that I believe your interest in buying the café is a viable option."

Her brows tented. "Um, last I heard, your parents are dead set on signing those papers."

"Exactly."

She lifted her coffee cup to her lips, staring at him over the rim as if he didn't make an ounce of sense.

Honestly, he couldn't fault her for being skeptical. His father came from a long line of stubborn folks. Tate held up his palm. "Hear me out, okay? I want to understand your plans so that when my dad comes home from fishing tonight, I'm prepared to have a meaningful conversation."

"Do you really think you can change his mind?"

Nope. "Absolutely." Tate flashed what he hoped was a confident smile. "I know I've been gone for a while, but I can tell by the way people have rallied around you that the café means something to this community and to you. It's worth saving."

She stood, then shoved her chair back under the table. "It seems your family hasn't quite come around to your way of thinking. Your mother could barely stand to speak to me."

Tate sighed. "Unfortunately, there's not a whole lot I can do about my mother's attitude. Come on." He pointed toward the door. "I'll finishing cleaning up, and then we'll walk over to the café. I want to hear more about your plans for the expansion."

"This is a waste of our time."

"If you want me to persuade my parents not to accept that offer, then I'm going to need a glimpse of your vision."

"Would you like to see my projected earnings and a formal business plan, too?"

He brushed past her and put the rest of the dishes in the dishwasher. "If you have that in writing, that would be great."

Don't let her sarcasm get you down. Sure, her concerns were as valid as her business plan, but her words still hurt. They used to have such an easygoing friendship. They'd rarely traded barbs like this in high school. He hated that he'd tarnished that with his choices.

Eliana retrieved her new artwork from the table. Tate dropped soap in the dispenser and started the dishwasher. He paused and flung a silent prayer toward heaven. *Please, please, let me not mess this up.*

She skirted the island, kids' artwork in hand and her expression unreadable. "Ready when you are."

"Great. Let's go." He checked to make sure his phone was in his back pocket so he could take notes, then followed her out of the apartment.

He squinted against the morning sunshine. Wispy clouds dotted the pale blue sky, and seagulls cried as they flew over the harbor. The familiar, pungent scents of fish and salt water greeted him as they walked down the stairs. He waved to his mom and the kids as she pulled out of the parking lot and drove away. Sure, coming home wasn't all rainbows and making memories, but he was determined to make the best of their circumstances.

Eliana followed him over to the café. Her silence ushered in a fresh wave of doubt. She obviously thought he was bonkers for doing this. He stopped at the edge of the lot and surveyed the building. Rocks anchored a blue tarp covering the giant hole in the structure. A remediation company's truck was backed up to the entrance, and the sound of industrial fans and dryers wafted from the open door.

It was easy to see why his parents wanted to sell, but he wouldn't let Eliana's dreams die that easily. He couldn't live with himself if he did.

"Tell me more about your plans." He pulled his phone from his pocket and opened the notes app.

She gave him a side-eye stare. "Are you really taking notes?"

"Why not? How am I going to persuade my parents to decline that offer if I don't come at them armed with facts?"

A smile played at the corner of her lips. The tightness in his chest loosened. If he made a highlight reel of his teenage years, almost every image would include Eliana and that gorgeous smile. He'd do just about anything to make her happy. To mend their fractured friendship.

This won't work. It's too little, too late.

He frowned. Mom's crummy attitude must've rubbed off. He gave the doubts a mental swat, but they still lingered, buzzing in his head like mosquitoes at a cookout. Would convincing his parents to change their minds be enough to erase the years of animosity between their families?

Why was he pretending to care?

Eliana's legs itched to run. She had to go. Somewhere. Anywhere but here. Because she couldn't handle watching him make her dreams his priority.

She scowled. His enthusiasm reminded her of a peppy high school cheerleader, and she was the grouchy hermit, squelching his positive attitude with her chilly cynicism.

"What's wrong?" Tate looked up from his phone. "Why are you getting upset?"

"I'm not." She pulled at her lower lip with her fingers. "It's…nothing. I'm fine. Really. I'm just— Since you don't need me here right now to watch the twins, I'll run a quick errand."

"But we're not finished." He gestured toward the café. "I thought you mentioned a fireplace?"

"Yep, a fireplace would be amazing." She walked backward toward her car, careful not to wrinkle the artwork she still clutched in her hand. "Don't worry, I'll pick the kids up from camp at noon. I promise."

"Eliana, wait. You don't have to go," he called after her. "What did I say?"

"Nothing." She forced a bright smile. "You know how it is when you think of something that you need to do, and you just want to get it done?"

Oh, brother. Flimsiest excuse ever.

"It can't wait?"

"No. Sorry." She waved. "I won't forget to pick up the twins. Thanks again for breakfast. See you." Turning away, she hurried to her car and slid behind the wheel.

Please, please don't follow me.

If Tate jogged toward her car right now and called her out on her faux-emergency errand, she'd only make a bigger fool of herself. If he turned those blue eyes her way and asked again what was really going on, she'd be forced to confess that she'd never gotten over him leaving the island.

Leaving *her.*

Yeah, it was sort of adorable how he took notes on his phone, but it didn't matter. She'd known Rex Adams her entire life, and he had never backed down from something once he decided it was a certain way. Her dreams for owning the café and its expansion had died when that tree fell through the roof.

She pulled her phone from her purse and sent all three of her sisters a text.

Emergency meeting at the Trading Post. My treat. Need help.

Dumping her phone in the cup holder, she started the car, then shifted into Reverse and pulled out of the parking lot. In the rearview mirror, she caught a glimpse of Tate still standing in front of the café, staring after her. She looked away. So he cared about her. That was sweet, but he had two little kids and a life in Boise. Sooner or later, he'd leave again, and she'd be left behind to sweep up the mess of her broken heart. No, thank you.

A few minutes later, she snagged the last empty parking space in the crowded lot behind the shops on Main Street. The Trading Post was a delightful coffee shop and souvenir stand on a busy street corner in the middle of Hearts Bay. Eliana's best friend, Annie, owned the business along with her parents. They'd named the place as a tribute to the Russian fur traders who'd visited Orca Island in the 1700s. The eclectic shop with its scrumptious baked goods, delicious coffee and unique souvenirs was a favorite of locals and tourists.

Eliana checked her phone as she exited the car. Her sisters, Rylee, Mia and Tess, had all texted back that they were on their way. She smiled at their prompt responses. They each had jobs and busy lives. It wasn't often that they could drop whatever they were doing and come to her rescue. Part of her wished she'd figured this out on her own, but she didn't want to. As the fourth of five children, she'd always looked to her family for guidance and support. It meant the world to her that they were all here on the island together. Even though Charlie's and Abner's deaths had left a huge crater in their lives, having her sisters close by had made the grief and loss more palatable.

The aroma of fresh-ground coffee beans mixed with the sweet scent of vanilla greeted her when she stepped inside the Trading Post. Annie smiled and waved from behind the espresso machine. Probably crafting another one of her trademark moose tracks mochas. Eliana's mouth watered at the thought of her favorite beverage, and she joined the line waiting to order.

Her younger sister, Rylee, waved from a table in the back corner. Exposed wood beams overhead, an overstuffed couch and two armchairs arranged near the gas fireplace, and small round tables dotting the eating area, encouraged customers to linger.

After Eliana placed her order with the college-aged boy Annie had hired for the summer, she joined Rylee. "Thanks for meeting me."

Rylee grinned. "I was already here when I got your text."

"I'm glad I caught you, then. Have you seen Mia or Tess?"

"Mia's in the restroom. Tess isn't here yet." Rylee's dark eyes sparkled with their usual mischievous gleam. "What's up?"

After Mia joined them and Annie delivered their drinks, Eliana shared a quick replay of her encounters with Tate and the twins. Whenever Tess showed up, she'd fill her in, too.

Frowning, Mia tucked a strand of her auburn hair

behind her ear, then slid her butter-yellow mug of chai closer. "That sounds like an intense reunion. I see why you're frazzled."

"I don't." Rylee pinched a corner off her chocolate chip scone. "Tell me again why this is an emergency? A nice guy wants to hear more about your interest in renovating a ruined building to your exact specifications, and now you're mad?"

"Wow, your empathy is remarkable." Eliana glared at her little sister. Sometimes Rylee's lack of a filter really stung. "Have you heard anything I've said? Tate's kindness isn't the issue."

"Then what is?" Rylee twisted the cardboard sleeve on her to-go cup in a slow circle. "Why are you so miffed that he wants to help?"

"Because his dad is never going to change his mind. He wants that building sold."

"But it's not a done deal. There's still time."

"Not enough."

"Anything could happen between now and Friday," Rylee insisted. "There's no harm in letting Tate speak to his parents on your behalf. I thought that's what you wanted?"

I did, too. Eliana sipped her drink, letting the warm coffee slide down her throat. But her reaction to Tate's kindness this morning rattled her. Provoked a seismic shift in her feelings. What if she got the café of her dreams but he hurt her again?

"Hey." Tess slid into the fourth empty chair at their table and peeled off her jacket. She flashed a tired smile. "Sorry I didn't get here sooner. I had to take Cameron to a playdate. What's going on?"

"Eliana's mad that Tate's doing exactly what she

wanted him to do," Rylee said, tacking a dramatic eye roll onto her summary.

"Careful, you'll hurt yourself rolling your eyes that hard." Eliana swallowed the caramel-and-chocolate-flavored coffee too quickly, wincing as it burned all the way down. "And please lower your voice. These walls have ears."

She cast a quick glance around the coffee shop. Every table except for one was filled, and two of Rex and Tammy's closest friends sat within earshot of her and her sisters.

"I'm going to need more tea for this one." Tess squeezed Eliana's arm. "I'd better go order. Hold that thought."

Mia sipped her tea, uncharacteristically quiet. Or maybe she couldn't squeeze a word in around Rylee's big opinions. "You haven't said much, Mia. What do you think about this whole mess?"

Mia hesitated.

Uh-oh. Eliana braced for more advice that she didn't want to hear.

"Let me ask you this." Mia's green eyes searched Eliana's face. "Is running that café really your dream? Or have you stayed on as manager because it's comfortable and you know what's expected?"

Eliana squirmed in her chair. "Why would you ask me that?"

"Because sometimes catastrophic events have a way of making us reevaluate what we truly want. That can be scary, especially if we've been hurt before." Mia's phone hummed, and she plucked it from her pocket. "I'm sorry, I have to go. I promised Mom I'd go with her to her doctor's appointment."

"Wait. What?" Rylee's worried gaze pinged between Eliana and Mia. "Why is she going to the doctor?"

Mia pushed back her chair, then hesitated. "I'm not sure if you've noticed, but she's been extra tired lately, had some frequent headaches, and Dad discovered some bruises on her legs."

Oh, dear. That was concerning. Why hadn't Mom said anything? "Please keep us posted," Eliana said. "And thanks for coming."

Rylee went to the restroom, and Tess stood at the counter, placing her order. Eliana stared after Mia as her oldest sister strode toward the door. She'd dismissed Mia's pointed question, but now the doubt wiggled in. The comment about catastrophes and reevaluating stuck with her like gum on the bottom of her shoe. And she didn't like it. Not one bit. Because operating a café in her own building was still her dream.

Wasn't it?

Chapter Five

$\mathbf{T}$ate lingered at the railing overlooking the boat harbor, silently rehearsing the speech he'd prepared. This was worse than when he'd asked Jade's father for permission to marry her. Wrapping his clammy palms around the metal railing, he closed his eyes and prayed.

Lord, please give me the words to persuade my father to change his mind. Soften his heart to accept a perspective other than his own, and please help me hold my temper if I don't like his answer. Amen.

He scanned the harbor and found his father's boat. Rex's broad shoulders and trademark black fleece vest layered over a long-sleeved white shirt were easy to spot. Tate wanted to make doubly sure today's guests had left, although he was pretty sure they had, because he'd passed Christian and Sarah a few minutes ago. They'd locked up the office just as he was leaving the apartment. The twins had been invited to a birthday party for a kid from their day camp. Tate had two hours free until he picked them up and absolutely zero excuses to avoid speaking with his father.

"Let's do this," he whispered, then strode down the ramp and onto the dock dividing the rows of boat slips.

"I know why you're here," Dad said when he saw Tate approaching. "The mayor already texted me."

Tate halted his steps near the bow of the boat. "I guess news still travels fast around here."

The crevices in Dad's brow deepened. Tate shifted from one foot to the other, swallowing against the dryness in his mouth. "What did Mr. Lovell have to say? If you don't mind me asking."

"Someone overheard Eliana and her sisters talking at the Trading Post this morning, so go on. Tell me what's on your mind."

"Have you ever taken the time to listen to Eliana's plans? She's given the expansion a lot of thought, and her ideas are incredible."

"I'm sure they are. But she could implement those plans of hers in another building." Rex angled the hose toward his boat's back deck and power washed the grit from the day's fishing charter into the harbor. Tate stood on the dock, his body itching to hop onboard and shut off the water. That would get his father's attention for sure. It would also mean sudden death for this conversation. Instead, he waited, hands on his hips, and studied his father's grim expression.

Come on. Give the girl a break. "She doesn't want another building. The café is well established in its current location."

Once the boat was scrubbed free of all the grime, Rex turned off the water and slowly recoiled the hose.

Maybe Eliana was right. Maybe this was a waste of time.

"What's in this for you, son?" Dad straightened, a muscle in his cheek twitching.

Tate opened his mouth to speak and then closed it again. He hadn't expected Dad to lead with that. "She's helping take care of Willow and Hunter. The café is closed because of that tree. A tree she asked you to take care of. The least we could do is—"

"Is that what this is about? She's mad that I didn't cut down that tree, so she sent you here to try and guilt me into declining that offer?"

Anger bubbled in his gut. "That's not what happened."

"Really?" Dad scoffed. "Help me understand why our family should turn down the opportunity of a lifetime so that a Madden can finally own that property."

Why did he have to twist his words and make Eliana sound so opportunistic? Tate looked away. "There's no reason for you to accept that deal, Dad. You know it will destroy this community."

"You're being a bit dramatic, don't you think?"

"And you're kidding yourself if you think it won't." Tate fought to keep his voice even. "A huge building will be an eyesore on this waterfront. I don't care who wants to get married in Hearts Bay, nobody needs a luxury hotel and a giant convention center for their wedding."

His father looked angry enough to spit nails. "Some would argue that nobody needs Eliana to own a nicer café, either, but here we are."

"Why are you so determined to crush her dreams? To prove a point? If this truly is about your and Mom's retirement dreams, then I'll back away. But if this is about revenge and one last shot at outdoing the Maddens, then I'm not going away quietly, because in that scenario, nobody wins."

Dad scowled. An icy river of regret washed down Tate's spine. So much for holding his temper. Calling out his father's intentions had clearly crossed an invisible line in their tenuous father-son relationship. An image of Eliana in tears as she stared at the tree lying across the café's roof flashed in his mind. He stood his ground. This wasn't high school. He was a grown man, not a teenager sneaking in late after curfew. His family had done enough harm to Eliana. It was time to break the vicious cycle and make the right choice.

Dad blew out a breath and sank onto the cooler behind him. "Here's the thing. The developer is more than likely going to back out on the offer, because the zoning change hasn't been approved. And I get that people are out of work because the café is closed. But they'll find other jobs, and in the long run, wouldn't selling our property finally put an end to this ridiculous feud between our families?"

"I don't understand." Tate leaned closer. "Are you saying that you're trying to be part of the solution?"

Rex smoothed his hand over his close-cropped hair. "I'm trying to be honest with you. Last I checked, this was a family business."

Tate gritted his teeth. Not a family business he was proud to be associated with. At least not right now.

"I anticipate more offers coming, but the council members have to approve the zoning change or else we're back to square one."

"And if they don't, then we'll start the repairs on the café?"

"We're not scheduling any repairs yet. I've got fishing charters booked solid for the rest of the summer, and your brother says he's starting a new job next week. Which means I'm down to one deckhand, and that's you."

Tate winced. "All right. I can make that work."

Dad frowned. "Tell Eliana that if the council rejects the zoning change, then I'll reconsider her offer."

Tate couldn't stop a smile. He jumped into the boat, his arms stretched wide. Dad's brow furrowed in confusion. Okay, so no hug then. Tate didn't let that dampen his excitement. He thrust out his hand. "Thank you."

His father's rough palm squeezed Tate's in a firm handshake. "You're welcome. I wouldn't start celebrating yet, though. Did you hear what I said? You have some long days on this boat ahead of you."

"Got it. Thanks."

If Dad was willingly sharing his intentions, maybe he wasn't out for revenge after all. Maybe he truly wanted to put an end to the Madden-versus-Adams feud, too. Tate clambered onto the dock and jogged toward the ramp, his boots clomping against the weathered wood. He fumbled in his pocket for his phone, but changed his mind. This wasn't the kind of announcement to share in a text. He wanted to tell Eliana himself. She'd need time to prepare her argument against the zoning change. And he wanted to do everything he could to help.

Baking her favorite dessert was supposed to distract her.

Instead, all she could think about was how she used to bake the decadent treats for Tate. She'd once failed an American history test because she'd stayed up too late baking him a pan of the seven-layer bars instead of studying. Throughout high school, she'd made it her mission to ensure Tate had double batches for basketball trips, his birthday and even his graduation party.

That was the last time she'd made him any seven-layer bars.

Plucking the bag of chocolate chips off the kitchen counter, she ripped the top open and poured straight from the bag into her mouth. Okay, a little extreme, but she'd eaten a salad for dinner. And burned plenty of calories playing hide-and-seek with the twins this afternoon. She deserved some chocolate.

The semisweet morsels did little to ease her convoluted emotions, though. Her encounter with Tate, followed by her coffee date with her sisters, had left her feeling confused. Owning the building had been her dream for so long. Why had Mia questioned that? If she couldn't keep working at the existing location, then she'd find a new venue. Open her own café. Rex Adams and those stupid trees were not going to be the end of her dream.

Unless she wasn't meant to work in the hospitality industry and this was the first step in a new direction. She gave her laptop on the kitchen table a sideways glance. A friend who'd moved to Washington and become a radiology technician had texted links to a few reputable programs. Eliana had visited the websites and looked over the application process but hadn't filled anything out yet. That was a big leap she didn't feel brave enough to take.

She added generous portions of chocolate and peanut butter chips to the graham cracker crust layered in the bottom of the nine-by-thirteen-inch pan. Nearby, her phone offered up one of her favorite songs from her country music playlist, and she danced toward the pantry to get a bag of shredded coconut. Her thick socks sent her sliding across the hardwood floor. Singing wasn't her gift, but that didn't stop her. She belted out the lyrics, ridiculously off-key. Ever since Tess had married Asher,

Eliana had been living alone. At first, she'd missed having a roommate, but now she appreciated the solitude.

A knock at the door threw her off her rhythm.

She sucked in a breath, pausing inside the pantry. Too bad the front porch wasn't visible from her hiding spot. She really didn't want to talk to anyone. The day had started so weird, with Tate's family fixing her breakfast and the twins presenting their homemade artwork apologies. She'd sidestepped another awkward interaction with Tate, but after a hectic afternoon with Willow and Hunter, she just wanted to recharge. Alone. Maybe even eat her favorite dessert straight from the pan once it came out of the oven.

Someone knocked again. Groaning, she tipped her head back and squeezed her eyes shut. Fine. Okay. She'd answer the door, then politely send her visitor on their merry way.

She left the pantry and moved toward the front door, grimacing at the folded laundry stacked on the back of her red sofa. An empty bowl, a mug and junk mail littered the coffee table. She wasn't exactly company ready. Whatever. Her surprise guest hadn't bothered to call first, so they were going to get an unfiltered look at her place. She reached for the knob but stopped and peeked through the narrow side window.

Tate stood on her porch, hands jammed in the pockets of his gray fleece pullover. She glanced down at the coconut in her hands, then looked around for some place to stash the bag. If he saw it, he'd know exactly what she was up to, and she wasn't ready to admit that she was making cookie bars and thinking about him.

"I know you're watching me." The corner of his mouth tipped up. "Open the door. I need to talk to you."

Ugh. Caught. Heat crept up her neck. She needed to learn to be more discreet. Unlocking the dead bolt, she pulled open the door. "Hey."

His gaze drifted to the coconut she'd tried hiding behind her back. "What have you got there?"

"Nothing."

"Is that coconut?"

"Maybe." She bit her lip, suddenly self-conscious in her well-loved black leggings and Charlie's faded Hearts Bay High T-shirt.

"Are you making seven-layer bars?"

"Yes. Why?"

His eyes shuttered, and he groaned. "Man, I love those."

She averted her gaze as Tate's reaction sent a feeling of warmth zinging through her. "Depending on what you have to say, maybe I'll bring you some tomorrow."

Oh, no. She clutched the bag tighter to keep from clamping her hand over her mouth. Poor choice of words. And that flirty tone in her voice. What had she done?

Tate's easy smile stretched wide, making her knees wobble. "What I'm about to tell you is definitely worthy of a seven-layer bar. Possibly even a whole pan."

"I'll be the judge of that." She stepped back and opened the door wider. "Come on in."

Tate followed her into the kitchen. She tossed the coconut on the counter, then leaned over and adjusted the volume on her phone. "What's up?"

Tate leaned against the door frame. "You might want to sit down."

She shot him an amused glance and tried not to think about how good he looked standing in her kitchen. "I can't sit down. I have to finish this dessert. Go on, I'm listening."

"Are you sure?"

"Absolutely." She tore the bag of coconut open, and Tate hesitated. Probably for dramatic effect.

"Okay, now you're making me nervous. Hurry up."

"The developer is more than likely going to back out on the deal if the zoning change doesn't happen. My dad's pushing for the town council to make the change, but he says if they vote against it, then he'll consider your offer."

The bag slipped from her hands, spilling flakes of coconut all over the counter. "You're kidding."

Tate's expression grew serious. "Eliana, this might be the break you need. What if you convince the council to vote against the zoning change?"

"They'll never listen," she whispered. "Your parents have way too much influence."

He closed the space between them in two long steps. "That is not true. You won't know until you try."

She shoveled the coconut into a neat pile with the side of her hand. "I admire your optimism, but that land is as good as sold." What was she supposed to do now? It was nice of Tate to share his parents' intentions, but the outcome would still be the same.

Wouldn't it?

"You can't let them win." Tate slipped his arms around her and gently pulled her into a hug.

She pressed her cheek against his chest and looped her arms around his waist. The warmth of his touch made her forget her bleak situation. For a few seconds, anyway. When she caught the familiar scent of his cologne, reality sank in. She froze.

But she didn't want to pull away.

His hands pressed against the small of her back. "You're going to get through this."

Tate's voice rumbled against her ear through the soft fleece of his pullover. If she lifted her head and tipped her chin up, she'd be dangerously close to his strong jaw, with that attractive stubble. And those lips she'd thought about kissing countless times.

It would be so easy to press onto her toes and—

No.

She took a giant step back and forced a smile. "Sorry. I get discouraged when I think about your parents getting exactly what they want."

"Don't be sorry." His voice was thick as his gaze held hers. "That place means a lot to you. My parents are blessed to have such a loyal manager, and it's a shame they are so focused on selling that they expect everyone to bend to their will."

"Exactly." *Then how long will it take for you to comply, too?* She twisted her fingers in the hem of her T-shirt, too afraid to ask. "It's getting late. Don't you have to pick up the twins from that birthday party?"

He glanced at the clock on her wall. "I'd better get going."

She followed him to the door. "Thanks for stopping by."

Oh, brother. He'd brought her intel on his parents' plans, hugged her and offered empathy, and all she could come up with was *thank you*?

He opened the door, then flashed her another smile over his shoulder. "You're welcome. I look forward to that batch of seven-layer bars."

She rolled her eyes. "Good night."

Once she'd closed the door behind him, she slumped

against it and sighed. Tate's news about the town council and the zoning change was encouraging. If the offer might fall through, then her dream wasn't completely dead. There was still a sliver of hope. As she returned to the kitchen to finish the dessert, instead of focusing on her future, her mind kept circling back to Tate and how good it had felt to be in his arms.

She quickly shoved the thought aside. They'd rekindled something that resembled friendship. That had to be enough. He'd kept his word and tried to help her, but that didn't mean he'd changed his mind about going back to Boise. Summer would be over in less than three months, and there was no point investing in a relationship that wouldn't last beyond Labor Day.

Tate hung up the phone, then double-checked the data he'd entered into the computer. Sarah had an errand to run and wanted to go home for lunch, so he was covering the fishing charter office. Just for today, though. Christian started his new job soon, which meant Tate would be Dad's only deckhand.

During a lull in the phone inquiries from potential customers, he'd collected the names, phone numbers and email addresses for Hearts Bay's town council. He couldn't stop thinking about Eliana's reaction to the news he'd shared last night. Or how good it had felt to hold her. Even for a few seconds. His parents' actions were hurting someone he'd cared for deeply. Someone he still cared about. And he wasn't going to stand back and let them win without a fight.

Except he hadn't figured out an effective way to intervene.

He blew out a long breath. This was getting complicated.

The door flew open, and Willow raced in. "Daddy, we're here."

"Hey, sweetie. How was camp?"

"Good." Her pink satchel bounced against her back as she darted around the desk. "Want to have lunch with us?"

He glanced toward Eliana, holding Hunter's hand. She was stunning. He couldn't look away. Or formulate an answer to Willow's question. Eliana's striped V-neck T-shirt and cropped jeans emphasized her petite frame. The sunshine behind her highlighted the coppery streaks in her long, dark hair.

"Daddy, we want to have lunch with you." Willow reached for his hand. "Come on."

Right on cue, his stomach rumbled. He was overdue for a lunch break. Grabbing something quick from a restaurant nearby and eating alone was the smarter choice, though. He couldn't share a meal with Eliana. Not right now. Not after last night.

He'd stopped by her place with the best of intentions to share the news that the zoning change had to be approved and the developer might back out if it wasn't. He'd wanted to offer hope. To encourage her that she could fight the change. When she'd obviously been discouraged, he'd pulled her into his arms. It was all he could do not to kiss her. And he couldn't kiss her. That would change everything. He had no plans to stay in Hearts Bay beyond August. The kids had to go back to Boise. *He* had to go back to Boise. Eliana's home was here. She'd never follow him out of the state. If he was honest, he'd wanted to be more than Eliana's friend back in high school. But he'd never acted on his feelings because his family would never approve of their relationship.

Although given his parents' recent behavior, he wasn't sure why he cared what they thought.

"I'm sorry we interrupted," Eliana said.

"You didn't interrupt." Tate stood and pocketed his phone. "I need to take a break for a few minutes, so I'll come up with you."

"Yay, you're coming." Willow grinned up at him. "Can we have grilled cheese sandwiches?"

He chuckled and tugged gently on one of her curls. "We'll see."

Hunter yawned and rubbed his eyes. "Will you carry me up the stairs? Please, Daddy?"

Tate traded an amused glance with Eliana. At least one of the kids would take an afternoon nap without putting up a fight.

"Sure thing." Tate scooped the little boy into his arms, then followed Eliana and Willow outside. "Did you have fun, buddy?"

"Not really." Hunter snuggled against Tate's shoulder. "I'm too tired to eat."

Tate hung the sign in the window with the little clock indicating they'd reopen at one thirty, then locked the door and pulled it shut. Willow giggled and ran toward the apartment's stairs. Hunter's whole body felt extra warm against Tate's as he hurried across the parking lot.

Willow delivered a play-by-play of the morning's events at camp. Eliana graciously listened, adding appropriate commentary whenever Willow took a breath.

Tate cupped his palm against the back of Hunter's head and slowly climbed the stairs. The boy's lack of interest in food worried him. Hunter might be a picky eater sometimes, but he rarely skipped a meal.

"Did you have a snack this morning?" Tate asked.

Hunter nodded, then shoved two fingers into his mouth. *Uh-oh.* The slurping on two fingers was a habit that had finally disappeared last year. He only reverted when he was super tired.

Inside, Eliana slipped out of her shoes, then hung up her coat. Willow ditched her bag, coat and shoes on the floor and raced toward the kitchen.

"Willow, come back and hang up your coat and bag, please." Tate sidestepped her belongings on his way to the sofa. "We don't leave our things lying on the floor."

"But, Daddy, I—"

"Willow, do not argue." Tate's words came out harsher than he intended, prompting Hunter to burst into tears.

Oh, no. Tate squeezed his eyes shut and lowered his son to the sofa cushions. "Hunter, I'm not upset with you."

"I don't feel good," Hunter wailed, curling into the cushions. "I'm cold."

"He cried two times." Willow held up two fingers on her return to the entryway, clearly pleased with herself for sharing this information. "And he said he wanted to go home."

Tate smoothed his palm over Hunter's forehead. Man, he was burning up.

"What can I do?" Eliana hovered behind the sofa. "Do you have a thermometer?"

"I didn't pack one." Tate gently lifted Hunter's head and tucked a throw pillow underneath. "There's some children's medicine in my shaving kit."

"Want me to get it?"

"If you could help Willow with her lunch, that would be awesome."

"Of course." She smiled, but her eyes were filled with concern. "C'mon, Willow. Do you still want a grilled cheese sandwich?"

"Yep." Willow skipped toward the kitchen. "And tomato soup."

"Do you have any?" Eliana trailed after her. "Let's look in the pantry."

"I want my jammies and a blanket," Hunter said, his teeth chattering.

"Let's go to your bedroom, and I'll help you change and get into bed."

Hunter sniffed then shook his head. "No, I want to stay here."

Resting on the sofa seemed unlikely with Willow bouncing around. Tate didn't have the heart to move him again, though. "I'll be right back."

He strode down the hall to the bedroom the kids shared. How had he missed that Hunter didn't feel well this morning? Too distracted about his plans for the day. Sick kids always made him feel so helpless. He hated that feeling.

Rummaging in the laundry basket full of unfolded clean clothes, he found a pair of Hunter's long-sleeve pajamas and matching pants. It wasn't the set with the race cars, which were his favorite, but those were still in the dirty laundry pile. At least these would help him get warm. Tate turned to leave, then remembered Hunter's blanket request. Tate plucked the cozy fleece one with the spaceships off the bed, along with Hunter's current favorite stuffed animal, a gray-and-white stuffed hippopotamus.

A loud clatter in the kitchen followed by glass shattering and Willow's screams punctuating the air sent him racing into the kitchen. "What happened?"

Eliana hunched over Willow on the floor, one hand on his little girl's forehead and the other caressing Willow's arm. "It's going to be all right, pumpkin."

Willow was sprawled on her back, blood trickling from her mouth. Shattered glass littered the floor around them.

A sour taste coated the back of his throat. He had to do something, but Willow's condition made him lightheaded.

Eliana glanced up at him, her brow furrowed. "We need to stop the bleeding."

"Don't move." He choked out the words then whirled in a circle. "The glass. I—I'll pick it up."

The broom. A dustpan. Maybe a Shop-Vac? Dad probably had all that stored in the closet downstairs. Panic sluiced through his veins. He had to think. Why couldn't he focus?

Hunter sat up and peered over the back of the sofa. "What happened, Daddy?"

"Sit tight, pal. I'll be right there."

"Tate." Eliana's voice drew his gaze to hers. "She needs medical attention. It's her—"

"My teeth!" Willow hollered. "Where are they?"

Eliana winced. "We're going to get you some help. Try to lie still for a minute." She smoothed Willow's curls back from her forehead. "Your dad and I are going to figure this out."

"What happened to her teeth?" He dropped Hunter's belongings on the counter and leaned closer. His legs wobbled, and his vision tunneled. He slowly sank to the ground.

Eliana's eyes grew wide. "Tate. You have to get her to the hospital. They'll bring in the dentist or whatever she needs."

"I know. You're right. It's just…there's all this glass and I'm not that great when…when there's blood."

Shame roiled his stomach. He should be stronger than this. Willow needed him.

"Daaddy," Hunter whined. "I need my hippo and my jammies."

"I—I know." Tate pushed to his feet, clutching the edge of the counter for support. "Give me a minute."

"Don't worry about the glass," Eliana said.

How was she staying so calm? "But you don't have shoes on."

"I'm a big girl. I'll figure it out. You need to get Willow in the car. *Now.*"

Eliana's firm tone spurred him into action. Thankfully, he still had his work boots on. Glass crunched under his soles as he crossed the small kitchen. "I'm here, sweetie. Let's get you to the hospital. Grandma's working today. She'll know what to do."

He gently lifted her into his arms. Willow cried out, clutching his shirt in her little hands. The blood on her face made him want to throw up, but he forced himself to focus. "It's going to be okay. I promise."

Eliana followed them to the door and yanked it open. "I'll stay with Hunter until you get back."

Tate paused in the doorway. "Thank you. For everything. You have no idea."

The tenderness in her eyes soothed the jagged, panicky feeling that tormented him. "No problem. Keep me posted."

* * *

Eliana sat in the recliner in the corner, a cup of coffee on the side table and a thriller novel she'd discovered on the bookshelf open in her lap. Tate and Willow were still at the hospital. Hunter slept on the sofa, the animated movie he'd insisted on watching playing quietly on the television.

Her phone hummed, alerting her to an incoming text. She glanced at the screen. Hoping for an update from Tate, she frowned at Annie's message.

We're still on for our marathon baking session tonight, right? Just double-checking that you're bringing the flour and the eggs.

Oh, no. Eliana stifled a groan. She'd completely forgotten that Annie had roped her into baking six dozen brownies for tomorrow's ribbon-cutting ceremony. The island's new Little League baseball field was finished. Mia's late fiancé, Abner, had been passionate about getting the field built, so the town council had voted to name it after him. In true Hearts Bay fashion, the ceremony included refreshments. Eliana had tried to convince Mia that she didn't have to help, but her sister had insisted. She'd appreciated that the community had rallied around her and their family after Abner and Charlie died. She was so touched by the decision to honor Abner's memory with the name of the field, how could she not play some small part in the celebration?

Eliana hadn't been able to argue with that. Annie had offered to host their brownie-baking session at the Trading Post, since she closed at five on Fridays and had plenty of space in her kitchen.

I'm still babysitting Hunter. Willow is at the emergency room with Tate. I'll be there as soon as I can.

She sent the text to Annie and waited for her response, which came quickly.

Oh, no. Sorry to hear about Willow. I hope everything's okay. Text me when you're on your way.

Eliana sent a quick reply, then left her phone on the table and took her coffee cup to the kitchen for a re-fill. The seven-layer bars she'd brought Tate sat on the counter untouched. After pouring more coffee into her mug and topping it off with creamer, she eyed the storage container again. He wouldn't notice if she ate one, would he? After all, she'd brought him the entire batch.

She quickly popped off the lid, selected one of the smaller pieces and carried her coffee and dessert over to the table. The first bite was as delicious as she remembered. Decadent and sweet. The layers offered the perfect combo of smooth and crunchy, salty and sweet, with the walnuts, coconuts and three kinds of candy.

Muffled footsteps on the stairs outside startled her. She glanced down at her half-finished treat. It was too rich to devour quickly, but she didn't want Tate to know that she'd pilfered from the batch she'd gifted him. And if Willow's arrival disturbed Hunter, they'd all be sorry. The boy needed his rest.

Pushing back her chair, she hurried to intercept them. When she got to the entryway, Tate and Willow had just come inside. Eliana pressed her finger to her lips. "Hunter's asleep," she whispered, angling her head toward the sofa. "How are you feeling, Willow?"

"My teeth are gone." Willow opened her mouth and pointed to the gap in the front.

Eliana gasped. "Where did they go?"

"Up." Willow clamped her mouth shut, then craned her neck to see the television. Probably wanted to make sure Hunter hadn't watched her favorite movie without her.

Eliana glanced at Tate for clarification. "Where are her teeth?"

"When she fell, she bumped her mouth on the counter, and somehow the force pushed her baby teeth up into her gums."

"Oh, wow." Eliana grimaced. "That must've hurt. You're so brave."

"Daddy, can I have ice cream now?"

Eliana smiled. Willow's exaggerated whisper made her lisp extra adorable.

"I promised her ice cream when we got home. Would you like some? It will go nicely with that chocolate you're eating."

Eliana touched the corners of her mouth.

He laughed. "Yes, you left the evidence on your face. I hope you weren't eating any of my seven-layer bars."

Heat rushed to her cheeks. "I only had one."

"I'm teasing." Tate squeezed her shoulder as he brushed past her. "You're entitled to more than one after all you've done for us."

Eliana followed him and Willow into the kitchen, her skin still tingling from the warmth of his touch. "It's no trouble. We agreed I'd watch your children, right?"

"Hang on, Willow." Tate ignored Eliana's comment and tugged his daughter closer. "There's broken glass in here, remember?"

"I cleaned it up," Eliana said. "Sarah came and stayed with Hunter for a few minutes while I went and got the vacuum from the café."

"Thank you." His appreciative expression made her want to come up with more reasons for him to look at her that way. "How is Hunter?"

"Much better now."

"Because he's sleeping?"

"Daddy." Willow pulled the freezer door open, took out the vanilla ice cream container and plunked it on the counter. "May I have some, please?"

Tate opened and closed two drawers before he found the ice cream scooper. "I'm working on it, sweetie."

"Can I watch a show, too?"

"Yes, but you need to go get the tablet on the dresser in my bedroom. You can sit right here in the kitchen and watch your show, because I don't want you to disturb Hunter."

"Oh-kayyy," Willow called over her shoulder as she skipped down the hallway toward the bedrooms.

Eliana reclaimed her seat at the table and reached for her coffee. "I found the medicine you mentioned and gave Hunter the dose listed on the container. He also wanted crackers and ginger ale. Hope I did the right thing."

Tate paused, a scoop full of ice cream suspended over a red plastic bowl. "You absolutely did the right thing. Went above and beyond, as far as I'm concerned. Sick kids are challenging, especially when they aren't yours."

Eliana looked away. Yes, he'd complimented her, but the reminder that he'd started a family with someone else resurfaced. The constant reminder of Jade's existence always seemed to hover.

"That's wild about Willow's injury." She forced the

conversation back to a topic that didn't make her insides twist into a jealous knot. "What did the doctor say about her permanent teeth?"

"That's what took so long." Tate brought Willow's ice cream to the table and set the bowl down. "We had to wait for the dentist to finish seeing his last patient before he could come to the emergency room. He says she'll get her permanent teeth like she's supposed to, and everything will be fine. I'm supposed to check inside her mouth and make sure she doesn't develop an abscess."

Willow returned with the device cradled to her chest. She sat down on the chair beside Eliana. "Want to watch a show with me?"

"I'd love to, but I need to get going. I need to help my friend Annie and my sister Mia do some baking."

Willow heaved a dramatic sigh. "See you."

Eliana stood and patted her shoulder. "I'm glad you're okay. I'll see you soon."

Tate brought Willow a spoon. "Here you go, sweetie."

She eyed the contents of the bowl. "No sprinkles?"

"I don't have any. Maybe we can get some the next time we go to the store."

Willow pooched out her lower lip, then shrugged and dug into her treat.

"I'll be right back," Tate said. "I'm going to walk Eliana out."

"I know the way." She picked up her napkin and coffee cup and carried them to the kitchen sink. Tate waited while she tossed her napkin in the garbage, then rinsed her mug and put it in the dishwasher.

He wasn't going to walk her all the way to her car. Was he? The weight of his gaze as she retrieved her phone from the living room sent a nervous tingle skipping across her skin.

Hands jammed in the back pockets of his jeans, Tate hovered by the door. She took her purse from the hook on the wall and slung it over her shoulder. "I'm so sorry about what happened. With Willow and her teeth. I should've been paying closer attention."

"She's fine." Tate offered a sheepish smile. "Thank you for remaining calm in a tense situation. This wasn't your fault."

"I still feel partly responsible." She shifted her weight from one foot to the other. "Next time, I won't turn my back on her."

"Don't be too hard on yourself." His eyebrows tented. "She already admitted that she was climbing on the counter, and she knows she isn't supposed to."

"I'm glad she's okay, and I hope Hunter feels better soon. Again, I'm sorry."

"Don't be. It was an accident. Thank you for staying with Hunter and taking care of him."

"Anytime." She turned and opened the door. "I'll see you Monday."

"Wait."

Oh, no. She needed to get going. Annie was already doing more than her share of the baking. Eliana faced him again.

"I was hoping I could see you this weekend." He ran his hands through his hair. "I have a list of the town council members and their contact info for you. We need to talk about your strategy for the meeting. You're going to prepare a speech, right?"

Oh. So he wasn't asking her out. She hoped her disappointment wasn't evident on her face. "Why don't you text me the information? I'm still thinking about what I want to say."

"Right. Of course." He reached past her for the door. "If you're baking for the ribbon-cutting ceremony, then I'm assuming you'll be there?"

She nodded.

His wide smile sent her pulse careening like a raft through white-water rapids. "Great. I'll see you then. Thanks again for everything."

"You're welcome." She forced the words from her dry mouth, then slipped outside. Taking the stairs two at a time, she hurried toward her car, eager to escape that way-too-domestic situation. If only she could shed her tangled emotions like a moose shed the velvet from his antlers. Scraped and scratched, an arduous but necessary process. She had to find a way to keep Tate and his beautiful children from taking up space in her heart.

Chapter Six

Hunter had monopolized Eliana's attention for far too long. Tate shouldn't have let that happen.

He shifted in his canvas chair and stole a glance at Eliana, determined to hatch a plan to get his son away from her. Hunter had snuggled up in her lap a few minutes ago. Before that, he'd sweet-talked her into taking him through the line snaking along the fence beside the baseball field. She'd returned to their circle of chairs carrying a plate loaded with a hot dog, a mound of chips and a brownie big enough for two people to share.

After mouthing *sorry* in Tate's direction, she'd shrugged and proceeded to let Hunter sit beside her while he devoured the whole thing. Yesterday's fever had sure disappeared in a hurry.

Chocolate and ketchup hugged the corners of Hunter's mouth. Judging by the heaviness of his eyelids, Tate predicted he had about three minutes to pluck his son off her lap and carry him to the car.

Except that meant ending an almost perfect evening.

Shades of orange and pink crisscrossed the pale blue sky. The sun glided toward the mountains, bathing the new baseball field in a soothing glow. Smoke from the charcoal fire curled into the air. Laughter punctuated the hum of conversation as people lingered, chatting in small groups. Dad and Christian sat nearby, trading good-natured barbs about the upcoming professional football season. Sarah entertained Willow with a bottle of bubbles.

The ribbon-cutting ceremony had officially morphed into Hearts Bay's version of a block party. Kids and grown-ups dotted the baseball field, playing catch and chasing each other around the bases. Someone had connected their phone to a wireless speaker, and familiar pop music filtered through the air.

Tate rubbed his palms on his jeans. If he didn't want to struggle with grumpy children tomorrow, he needed to get the twins home for baths and bedtime. He shot Eliana another glance. She didn't flinch when Hunter draped his undoubtedly sticky hands around her neck and snuggled closer.

Man, he needed to go back to Idaho before they all became even more attached. Sure, Jade had given her blessing to a summer in Alaska, but she hadn't agreed to anything permanent. Besides, their custody arrangement was fifty-fifty. A legal document prevented him or Jade from moving out of state and taking the kids. Even though their marriage hadn't lasted, Jade needed to see the twins on a regular basis. Willow and Hunter needed their mother.

Eliana lifted her chin and caught him staring. A feeling of warmth ignited in his chest and spread through his extremities. She held his gaze, then shifted her attention back to Hunter. The kid had fallen asleep.

Staring at Eliana nestled in her camp chair with

Hunter asleep in her arms sent his mind sprinting ahead. Imagining scenarios where he had a future with her.

"Daddy." Willow cupped her hands around her mouth and called to him in an exaggerated whisper. "Hunter is asleep."

"Yeah, I noticed. Guess Eliana and Hunter are sleeping out here tonight." He winked at Eliana, earning him a sweet smile. Maybe tomorrow he should thank Hunter for falling asleep. He couldn't get enough of staring at her with his son in her arms.

"Can I sleep out here, too?" Willow abandoned her bubbles with Sarah and ran toward him. "Please?"

"I was kidding, sweetie. Nobody is sleeping at the baseball fields."

Willow's shoulders sagged, and her eyes filled with tears.

"The mosquitoes will eat you up." Eliana gently tugged on one of Willow's pigtails. "We can't have that."

"We could camp. Does Grandma have a tent?"

Tate stifled a groan. Setting up a tent in his parents' yard, dragging out sleeping bags and mattress pads, then getting the kids settled was a nightmare. He hadn't recovered from the last time they'd tried to camp in their backyard in Idaho almost a year ago.

"I'm going to ask Grandma and Grandpa if we can stay at their house tonight." Willow ran off before Tate could stop her.

"Willow, wait." He stood and pulled his phone from his pocket. Thankfully, he could text faster than she could move. He quickly sent a text warning Mom of Willow's spontaneous notion, then watched as his mother stopped her conversation with a friend near the dessert table to glance at her phone.

She smiled, her fingers moving quickly over the device, as Willow reached her side.

His phone hummed with an incoming text message.

Sounds great. You could probably use a night off. We are ready when you are.

Huh. That wasn't the answer he'd anticipated. His parents' willingness to help him out eliminated the stress of taking overstimulated kids home to the apartment and putting them to bed by himself. He tucked his phone back in his pocket and turned toward Eliana.

"What's going on?" She shifted in her chair, carefully adjusting Hunter's position on her lap. He sighed but didn't wake up.

"Willow persuaded my mother to let her stay over."

"Hunter, too?"

Tate nodded and collapsed the red canvas chair. "Let me put a few things in my parents' car, then I'll be back to get Hunter."

"Take your time."

That was the thing. He didn't want to take his time. Every minute spent getting Hunter and Willow situated meant less time alone with Eliana. Call him selfish, but the minutes were fleeting. Summer was flying by. He couldn't change the fact that he'd never told Eliana how much he liked her. Or confessed that he'd let their complicated family dispute influence his decision to choose Jade over her. And he certainly owed her an explanation. But the more time they spent together, the more he found himself hoping that their fragile bond might develop into something more.

Mom stood waiting by her SUV, Willow's hand

clasped in hers. She offered an encouraging smile. "I'm happy to take Hunter to our house if you'll transfer him to the car seat. I bought and installed two, by the way. Figured I'd be driving them around a lot this summer."

He wanted to hug her. "Thank you, Mom. I couldn't do this without you."

"Sometimes we have to work together." She glanced down at Willow. "Right, pumpkin? You're going to help me get everything we need for a sleepover."

Willow's gap-toothed smile made his mother chuckle. "Except I have a question." Willow's expression morphed into a frown. "Daddy, is Eliana keeping Hunter?"

"Nope, he's going with you and Grandma. Give me a minute." He set the chair on the ground by the truck he'd borrowed from Christian and retraced his steps to Eliana. After he settled Hunter in the car seat in Mom's vehicle, he'd be kid-free for the night. It had been weeks since the twins had spent a night away from him. As he met Eliana's gaze, thoughts of driving her home quickened his steps. Now he just had to convince her to leave with him instead of Annie or Mia.

She should've driven separately. Or caught a ride home with her parents. Somehow everyone in her family had already left the ribbon-cutting ceremony without her noticing. Until now. She turned in a slow circle to find Annie. Her bestie sat in a canvas chair near the ball field's chain-link fence, deep in conversation with a guy Eliana had never met. Everything about her body language indicated she had no intention of leaving any time soon. Super.

"I can give you a ride home." Tate took the empty brownie containers from her hands. "It's no trouble."

No trouble for you.

She wiped her clammy palms on her jeans and reached for her purse. Yeah, okay, maybe her reaction was juvenile, but being alone with him made her nervous. The kids always provided a buffer. She was already teetering on the precipice of falling in love with him again. Which was ridiculous, because he was still leaving at the end of the summer. The twins had to start school, and he probably had houses to build. Besides, Willow and Hunter needed to be with their mother. This arrangement between Eliana and Tate wouldn't last. Her job was to get them through the next six weeks safely, then say goodbye. The thought planted a hollow ache in her chest. Willow and Hunter tested her patience, but she'd miss them when they were gone.

"Eliana?" Tate's deep voice pulled her back to the present. "Would you like a ride?"

She nodded, then followed him toward the silver truck he'd borrowed from Christian for the summer. A short fifteen-minute drive. Surely she could handle that?

The familiar smells of Tate and spruce trees, mixed with a hint of leather and sawdust, hung in the air. She slammed the door and waited for him to circle around to the driver's side. He stowed the containers in the cab, then climbed behind the wheel and flashed her smile. "This is like old times, right?"

"Uh-huh." She barely squeaked out the words. And just like old times, her mind teased her with a scenario she couldn't allow to become reality. She'd scoot over and sit as close as possible. Her shoulder would press against his. Maybe he'd drape his arm across the back of the seat and play with her hair—

Stop. It. She squeezed her eyes shut to block the notion

before her imagination created any more impossible-to-resist scenarios. Thankfully this was a newer model and the truck had a substantial center console, keeping her firmly separated from him.

Good. That was for the best.

"Thanks for hanging out with us tonight." Tate put the key in the ignition and started the engine. She locked her seat belt in place. Yet another measure designed to keep her from touching him.

He glanced over his shoulder before shifting into Reverse. "Sorry about Hunter."

"What are you apologizing for?"

Tate's gaze lingered on hers. Eyes that blue should really be illegal. "He got a little too comfortable. Pretty sure he got chocolate or ketchup on your clothes."

She chuckled. "Don't worry about it. I'm washable. He's such a sweet boy."

"Yes, and a breath of fresh air in comparison to his sister." He puffed his cheeks, blew out a long breath and drove out of the parking lot.

"I admire her grit," Eliana said. "That confidence will take her places in life."

"Days like today make me thankful for you and my parents. Some nights bedtime with twins is a mountain I can't climb alone."

She let his comment linger. So he was grateful for her. But was he concerned about her attachment to his kids? The question hovered on the tip of her tongue. She wasn't brave enough to ask, though. Mostly because she didn't want to hear his honest answer.

Tate braked at the stop sign beside the exit, checked both directions, then turned onto the two-lane road highway that hugged the island's coast.

"Willow and Hunter seem to be having a good time here," she said, desperate to fill the silence and prevent her mind from dwelling on a future that simply wasn't possible.

"They wouldn't be having nearly as much fun if they didn't have you to hang out with." He shot her another one of those heart-stopping smiles. "Thank you for making sure they have a wonderful summer here."

"I have to admit I was skeptical at first, since kids really aren't my thing, but they are a lot of fun."

"You know, you keep saying that kids aren't your thing. I don't buy it." Tate's hand left the wheel and rubbed his smooth jaw. She tried not to trace the path of his fingers with her eyes. Forcing herself to look away, she stared straight ahead through the windshield. The sun wouldn't set for another three hours, giving the island residents a solid twenty-two hours of daylight to enjoy. As it inched closer to the horizon, its bronze light bathed the rolling hills in the middle of the island a brilliant purple. Across the water, Mount Larsen stood dark against a coral-and-pale-blue sky. Man, she loved this view.

"If you weren't running the café, what would you be doing for a living?"

Her breath hitched. Mia's question from their chat in the coffee shop resurfaced. *Is running that café really your dream?*

"You're the second person to ask me that lately." She played with the closure on her purse, twisting it open and closed. "Given recent events, maybe I should have a plan B."

Tate studied her. "There are no rules here. You don't have to commit to anything. We're just having a conversation."

She stared at the floorboards, scraping the toe of her ankle boot against the pebbles dotting the mat. "Before the Johnsons moved and I took over managing the café, I'd thought about becoming a radiology technician. My parents encouraged me to have a plan in case—"

"Hold on." He braked hard, and she glanced up, bracing her hand on the dashboard. The truck rolled to a stop a few feet away from a mama moose and her two calves ambling across the highway. Their chocolate-brown fur and long, spindly legs made Eliana smile. Once they were safely in the trees off the edge of the highway, Tate slowly sped up.

"Too bad Willow's not here." Eliana shifted in her seat. "She keeps asking when she'll see a baby moose."

"I'm quite thankful she's not here," Tate said. "She'd beg me to stop and take pictures."

"I don't know if we'll see any animals, but I'd like to take them on a few short hikes. Assuming you're okay with that?"

Tate nodded. "Be careful. You know the saying—this island has more brown bears than people."

"Since they're only four, we won't go far. I'll check with my brother-in-law, Asher, for some tips about the best trails. He spends a lot of time monitoring the island's wildlife population."

"Sounds good. Let me know when you decide to go."

They rode in silence until Tate pulled up in front of her house. He parked and turned off the engine. She reached for the door handle, but didn't climb out. "Thanks for the ride home."

"You're welcome." He searched her face, his gaze lingering on her lips. She angled her body toward his. Her heart hammered. Oh, she'd dreamed of this moment when they were in high school. Imagined sharing good-night kisses that threatened to make her late for her cur-few. Tate moved closer, leaning one elbow on the console. She stared into his blue eyes, which had darkened to a smoldering shade she couldn't quite name. Indigo? And those lashes. Long and dark. So not fair.

He tipped his head slightly, then hesitated, waiting for permission. Or giving her the opportunity to leave.

But she couldn't. An invisible magnetic force tugged them together.

Bridging the last remaining gap, she closed her eyes and pressed her lips to his. Tate didn't respond at first, and her stomach plummeted. What if he didn't want her? What if she'd misread the moment? Then he cupped her cheek with his callused fingertips. Her worries vanished as he returned the kiss. Soft and slow.

She tasted remnants of chocolate and salt. Skimming her palm up his arm and across his shoulder, she let her fingers rest in the hair at the base of his neck. Kissing Tate was better than she'd imagined, and she didn't want to stop.

But she had to. What had gotten into her? This was a huge mistake. She pulled away.

Tate's eyes sprang open. A smile spread across his handsome features. "That was—"

"I'm sorry. I shouldn't have done that. I—I have to go." She grabbed her purse and pushed the door open.

"Eliana, wait."

She hopped out of the truck and slammed the door, then jogged toward the house before she changed her mind and turned back. No matter how much she'd en-joyed that kiss, it didn't mean anything. His parents would never stand for their son falling in love with a

Madden. Besides, Tate, Willow and Hunter were not stay-ing in Hearts Bay. The twins belonged in Boise with both of their parents and their stepfather. She wasn't willing to let Tate break her heart all over again. Maybe she didn't have a solid backup plan if the café never reopened, but a broken heart was one scenario for her future that she refused to accept.

"I get to talk to Mommy first."

"No, I do." Hunter pushed his way between Willow and the coffee table. "It's my turn."

"Guys, take it easy." Tate scooted forward on the sofa and gently separated them. "There will be plenty of time to chat with Mommy. Let's call her."

He anchored his device on its stand in the middle of the coffee table and selected Jade's number from the list of contacts. Hunter sank onto the cushions beside him and leaned his head on Tate's shoulder. Willow stood be-side him, one hand on his knee and her eyes riveted on the screen. The familiar sound of the video call bubbled from the device's speaker.

Please answer, he silently pleaded. These Sunday-afternoon video calls had been Jade's idea, but so far she'd spent every single one examining her fingernails, sighing loudly and interrupting the kids' stories. They both were still eager to talk to her, though, so he'd hon-ored the commitment.

"Is she there?" Hunter pushed two of his fingers into his mouth. The stuffed hippo was tucked under his other arm.

Willow leaned against him. "Why won't she answer, Daddy?"

Thankfully he didn't have to make up excuses. Jade's

face appeared on the screen. Hunter pulled his fingers from his mouth and pointed. "Mommy. Hi, Mommy."

"Do you like my dress?" Willow pointed to her lavender cotton dress adorned with a popular kitty pattern and twisted side to side.

Please compliment her, or she'll be crushed. Tate tried to convey his wishes to Jade with a meaningful stare. She refused to look at him, though, and her brittle smile made him grit his teeth.

Hunter leaned toward the device, determined not to be upstaged. "Mommy, guess what? We camped last night in a tent. It was epic."

Jade's pencil-thin brows disappeared beneath her blond bangs. "You camped. *Outside?*"

Tate pressed his lips together to keep from laughing. Her disgust about anything outdoorsy hadn't changed.

"And we had hot dogs, potato chips and brownies for dinner," Willow added. "The brownies were so good that I had two."

Jade's disapproving gaze toggled to him. "Tate, really? Is that your idea of a healthy dinner?"

Oh, that was ironic coming from a woman who always made everyone else provide the meals for children. "We were at a party. Don't worry, I'll feed them plenty of grapes and carrot sticks with their organic chicken nuggets for dinner."

Hunter gasped. "We're having chicken nuggets for dinner? Yummy."

Jade's frigid gaze shifted back to Willow. "Why are you talking like that? Did something happen to your teeth?"

Willow looked up at him with panic swimming in her eyes.

"I called you from the ER." He leaned closer to the camera and kept his voice even. "When you didn't answer, I left a voice mail. You never called me back."

She quirked her lips to one side but didn't argue. He'd followed up with a text message, which she had also ignored. No point in mentioning that now. Her excuses wouldn't change anything.

Jade sighed and examined her nails. "So what happened?"

"Willow fell and bumped her mouth on the kitchen counter." Tate gently rubbed Willow's backside, hoping to soothe her anxiety. "The dentist said we'll need to wait for her teeth to reemerge, and this shouldn't impact her permanent teeth."

"Unless I get an access, remember?"

Tate kissed the top of her head. The mispronunciation was too cute to correct. "That's right, you could still get an infection. If that happens, the dentist will know what to do."

"Oh, my sweet baby." Jade pressed her manicured fingertips to her mouth. "That sounds awful. Tate, do I need to come up there? Are you sure this little adventure of yours is a good idea?"

He wiped his palm down his face. She wasn't going to get under his skin. Not this time. "This summer adventure was your idea, remember? Accidents happen. Kids get hurt. It's not a big deal."

"I'm concerned they're not getting proper supervision." Jade sniffed. "Who's watching them if she fell and knocked out her teeth?"

"My teeth are still here." Willow opened her mouth wide and pointed. "You can't see them right now."

"Mommy, guess what?" Hunter squeezed past Tate's

knees and stepped in front of the camera. "I had a fever and Eliana watched me. She gave me crackers and ginger ale."

Oh, no. Tate swallowed back a groan.

Jade paused, the plastic tumbler in her hand halfway to her mouth. "Who is Eliana?"

"She's our babysitter, and she's super fun to play with." Hunter jiggled his stuffed animal at the camera, obviously quite pleased with himself for adding to the conversation.

"You have a babysitter?" Jade's voice dripped with disdain. "Why?"

"Only part of the time," Willow said. "In the mornings we go to camp, because Daddy has to work."

Tate clasped Hunter's arm and gently lowered the stuffed animal so he could still make eye contact with his ex-wife. "Jade, I—"

"No, it's fine. I completely understand." Her expression indicated she didn't understand at all. "I'm happy to hear the three of you are getting so much quality time together."

Oh, brother. Before he could respond, the muffled sound of the doorbell ringing in the background drew her attention away from the screen.

"I have to cut this short." She didn't bother to conceal her excitement. "A friend of mine is coming by. Chad and I are going to redecorate the house, and I wanted to get her opinion on a few things."

"No," Hunter whispered. "Not my room."

"Not mine, either," Willow wailed. "Please, Mommy, no."

Tate fisted his hands in his lap. What a lousy way to

share her redecorating plans with the kids. Hadn't they experienced enough change lately?

"We'll talk about it when you get home, darlings." She blew kisses toward the camera. "Love you. Bye-bye."

She ended the call without waiting for a response. Tate jabbed the power button and the screen went dark. Willow and Hunter burst into tears.

"It's going to be all right." Tate rubbed both their backs with his palms. They cried louder, and he struggled to come up with anything comforting to say. Jade did whatever she wanted and gave little thought to their preferences. So infuriating. He hadn't been this angry with her in a long time. She'd spent every single call behaving like she'd rather have bamboo shoots jammed under her fingernails than talk to her own children. It was all he could do not to call her back and share a few choice words.

"Come here, kiddos." He pulled Willow and Hunter into his arms. "That was a rough one, huh?"

Hunter nodded, his little body trembling as he drew a gulp of air.

"She doesn't listen," Willow sobbed, dragging the sleeve of her dress under her nose.

"Shh," Tate whispered, planting another kiss on her forehead. "Your mommy and I love you both very much."

Willow buried her face in his shirt. She'd spent at least thirty minutes picking out her outfit before they'd called Jade, and she'd begged Tate to help her fix her hair. He'd done his best, although the result wasn't great. The headband she wore with the oversize bow camouflaged most of the tangles, anyway.

"I didn't get to tell her what I want for my birthday," Hunter whispered.

"Don't worry, your birthday is still a few weeks away." Tate hugged him close. "I'll make sure Mommy knows what you want."

"Where is Eliana?" Willow sat up and slid from his lap. "She listens. She'll make this better."

"Um, I'm not sure." Tate looked around for his phone. Willow was right. Eliana would know how to soften the blow of Jade's careless actions.

"Yeah, Eliana makes everything better." Hunter squeezed his beloved hippopotamus tighter. "Can you text her? She might bring us chocolate milk."

Tate couldn't stop his smile. "Good listening skills and great snacks—that's solid criteria for a wonderful… friend."

Was that what she was? A friend? That was how he'd always regarded her, but yesterday's kiss had changed everything.

Hunter's face puckered. "Cry-what?"

"Nothing, never mind." Tate rubbed the top of Hunter's head. "It's Sunday, guys. She's probably relaxing and hanging out with her family."

"We can relax and hang out," Hunter said.

"How about we play a game?" Tate pointed toward the small stack on the bookshelf. "We have some of your favorites here."

Willow shook her head. The giant bow flopped up and down. "We want Eliana. Call her. Please."

Tate hesitated. After they'd kissed, Eliana had jumped out of the truck and run to her house. Not exactly the body language of someone who was eager to hear from him. He was no match for Willow and Hunter's teary-eyed gazes, though.

"All right." He found his phone under a magazine on the coffee table. "I'll send her a text right now."

Hey, the kids and I wanted to know if you're busy tonight? We're planning on a gourmet meal of chicken nuggets, carrot sticks and grapes. Would you like to join us?

He sent the text, and they all hovered over his phone, staring at the screen. What if she didn't respond?

"I hope she says yes." Hunter slurped on his fingers again. His and Willow's heads were so close together they almost touched. Finally, the three dancing dots appeared as Eliana typed her response.

Tate held his breath. What if she said no?

Thank you for thinking of me. Sounds delicious! I'm going to sit this one out. See you tomorrow.

"What does it say?" Willow rocked Tate's knee back and forth. "Is she coming over?"

He sighed. "Sorry, kiddos. She can't make it. We'll see her tomorrow, though."

"Oh-kay." Hunter frowned. "Can we eat now?"

"I'm not hungry." Willow flopped on the sofa. "Can I watch a movie?"

"Sure." Tate stood and retrieved a fleece blanket she'd discarded earlier on the floor and tucked it around her. He found another blanket for Hunter and helped him get comfortable on the other end of the sofa. After they agreed on an animated favorite, Tate streamed the movie on the television, then went to the kitchen to fix dinner. He couldn't decide which bothered him more—Jade's upsetting conversation or the fact that the twins were bummed they couldn't hang out with Eliana. To be honest, he was bummed, too. Which confirmed his new reality. He wanted to be more than just her friend.

Chapter Seven

Eliana took the turn into the parking lot in front of the café too quickly, earning her a curious glance from Rex and a disapproving glare from Tammy. Of course they were already here, right on time. Four town council members were also present. Super. She would've missed this meeting completely if Annie hadn't heard about it at the Trading Post and sent her a text.

"This morning is off to a great start," she grumbled, angling her car toward her usual spot at the far end of the building. A dense, misty fog had rolled in off the water and clung to the rooflines. How fitting—weather that matched her mood. She turned off the ignition, then flipped down the visor mirror to assess her appearance. The circles under her eyes and pillow indentation on her cheek made her grimace.

"Frazzled with a side of exhaustion. So attractive."

She had only herself to blame. The latest news regarding her mother's health was troubling. Mia and Dr. Rasmussen both believed she needed further testing in Anchorage or possibly Seattle. Add that to her growing list of complicated feelings. After kissing Tate, she'd tossed and turned for two nights in a row, regretting her choices. Or at least trying to pretend she regretted that one particular choice. The softness of Tate's lips and the sensation of his fingers caressing her cheek were impossible to forget. Their first kiss had been incredible, but it couldn't erase her concerns about a romantic relationship.

They still wanted different things.

Didn't they?

She flipped the visor up, dropped her keys in her purse and grabbed her coffee.

"Good morning," Rex greeted her when she climbed out of the car. "Glad you could make it."

Wait. He was? The unusually polite comment made her already nervous insides dip and sway. She nudged the door shut with her hip and formed her mouth into a smile. "Sorry I'm late."

Lost too much sleep thinking about your son.

The inappropriate thought almost spurred a nervous cackle. She tamped it down with a generous sip of her coffee.

"No problem," Tammy said. Her thin smile was anything but forgiving.

Against her better judgment, Eliana fired a panicked look toward the door of the apartment. Surely Tate would join them before her conversation with his parents grew even more awkward.

"Tate stayed upstairs with the twins." Tammy fixed Eliana with a knowing stare. "Hunter is still sleeping, and Willow's eating breakfast."

"Thank you for the update." Eliana zipped her jacket against the damp morning air seeping around her, then offered a polite smile to the council members quietly observing their interaction. "Good morning."

"Don't worry." Rex jangled his keys in his hand. "I'll bring Tate up to speed later. We wanted to meet briefly and get everyone on the same page."

Right. Eliana bit her lip to keep from saying something foolish and followed Rex toward the café's front door.

Let it go. You've got to stay focused and ask for what you want.

What she wanted was the café reopened. Peak tourist season was galloping by. Didn't Rex and Tammy care about all the lost revenue? Most of the other employees had found new jobs. Technically she had, too, since she'd started babysitting the twins. But it wasn't the same. She missed her routine and connecting with her favorite customers.

Why were they determined to close one of Hearts Bay's beloved venues? Her stomach twisted. The expressions on the council members' faces and Tammy's demeanor didn't inspire confidence. Had they already made up their minds?

Rex pushed a key into the lock and opened the door. When she stepped inside, the familiar fragrance of the vanilla-scented air freshener greeted her.

The dark interior, chairs stacked on tabletops and tarps draped over the counter made her legs feel like limp noodles. She should be making coffee, pulling the till from the safe in the back office, double-checking that salt and pepper shakers were filled. Anthony and his helper would already be in the kitchen prepping for the morning rush. Instead, the stools sat empty and the whole place felt sad.

The council members, Rex, Tammy and Eliana stood in a semicircle.

"As you can see, the damage from the storm is extensive." Rex turned on his phone's flashlight and shined it around the restaurant. "My family and I don't feel the need to invest in repairs when a future owner will likely destroy the building."

Eliana gasped. "We haven't even had a meeting about a zoning change yet. What about community input? A hotel and a convention center will have a huge impact on parking, traffic, the environment. Shouldn't the people of Hearts Bay have a say in this?" Her voice sounded like she'd swallowed gravel. She cleared her throat and looked every single person in the eye. "There's still time for you to act, as council members and citizens. Please don't let this beautiful waterfront be destroyed for the sake of progress and the Adamses' retirement plans."

Rex and Tammy exchanged glances. The council members shifted awkwardly, then looked toward Mayor Lovell for guidance.

Mayor Lovell frowned. "She makes a valid point. The purpose of this morning's gathering is an informal look at the state of the café, not for both parties to campaign for their position on the argument."

Heat flushed her cheeks. If she didn't speak up, who would? There wasn't anyone else here to challenge Rex and Tammy.

"We need to mention the scope of the repairs would require a substantial renovation." Tammy turned in a slow circle. "The insurance company made a fair estimate for the damage from the tree, and they've released the first payment, but they won't cover anything that they consider an upgrade. That's why it's in our best interests to sell."

"Exactly. *Your* best interests, but it's not what's best

for Hearts Bay." Eliana fumbled in her purse for a spread-sheet she'd pulled together and handed it over. "Here's a list of everything I feel needs to be done, based on my experience as the café's manager, including estimated costs. If Tate is charging for labor, we'll have to add that in. I'm assuming that would be an additional twenty percent."

Scanning the paper, Rex released a low whistle. "This is quite thorough."

The divot in Tammy's brow deepened. "These are substantial improvements. How do you propose we pay for this? I'm not interested in a construction loan."

"Cash."

Tammy barked out a laugh. "That's cute."

Rex put his hand on her arm. "Take it easy, hon. Let's hear what she has to say."

"My sisters and I split Charlie's assets four ways. If you sell the property to me, I'd cover the cost of the improvements. Or we could negotiate on the price of the sale."

Tammy's eyes rounded. "Surely he didn't leave you enough to—"

"He had a lucrative business as a commercial fisherman before he passed away." Eliana fought to keep the tremor from her voice. Tammy's judgmental attitude grated on her nerves. "I'm prepared to make you an offer on the building and the land, but if you're not interested in selling to me and the council votes against the zoning change, when you choose to sell in the future, surely you'll recoup your investment."

Wow. Where did *that* come from? Yeah, okay, so she'd rehearsed these ideas in her head while staring at her ceiling in the middle of the night, but she hadn't said them aloud. To anyone. Her mouth ran dry. Had she made the best possible offer? What if they refused? And if they said yes and she bought the building, would she have the courage to follow through? Was this still her dream?

He had never in his life wanted a sleeping child to wake up more than he did right now. Tate hovered in the hallway outside Willow and Hunter's bedroom and peered through the gap provided by the slightly open door.

"Come on, wake up," he whispered.

Hunter didn't move. The blankets were pulled up to his ears. Only a shock of curly honey-blond hair was visible against the backdrop of his bright blue pillowcase.

Tate backtracked to the living room. He'd give Hunter twenty more minutes. If the kid slept much later, there wouldn't be time for him to eat breakfast before camp started. Eliana had agreed to drop the twins off today because Tate had a fishing charter.

Willow sat on the carpet beside the coffee table, flipping through a children's book. Eliana's sister Tess had sent over a tote bag full of books for the twins to borrow. He hated to interrupt her reading, but if she didn't get out of those pajamas and into her clothes for camp, she wouldn't be ready in time, either.

"Willow, you need to get dressed. Go pick your outfit, please." He opened their backpacks leaning against the back of the sofa and double-checked to make sure he'd remembered snacks, water bottles, swimsuits and towels. Today the campers were meeting at the high school to swim in the pool for a couple of hours. He didn't want to overlook anything they might need.

"Sweetie, did you hear me? Time to get ready."

She heaved a sigh and set the book aside, then took

a long pull from the straw in her pink-and-white plastic cup.

Uh-oh. Everything about her body language telegraphed her lack of excitement. Weird. Back in Boise, she loved going to the pool. After her last session of swim lessons, she'd begged to go again. He zipped up the backpacks, then moved around the end of the sofa.

"What's going on, pumpkin?" He dropped to the floor beside her. "You seem bummed."

She hung her head.

"You can tell me. I promise I won't be upset."

"I don't want to go swimming." Her voice was barely audible. She refused to look at him.

Before he could ask why, the door opened and Eliana stepped inside. A ribbon of damp, cool air flowed in behind her, and Willow shivered.

"Oh." Eliana hesitated in the doorway. "I'm sorry, I should've knocked first."

"You don't have to apologize. We were expecting you." Tate motioned for her to join them. "Come on in."

Eliana closed the door and shrugged out of her blue anorak. He felt his shoulders sag with relief, not just because she was here and could help him figure out what to do for Willow, but also because he couldn't wait to hear what had happened with his parents and the council members who'd showed up outside the café this morning.

Eliana hung up her coat and purse, then slipped off her shoes. When she faced them, her dark eyes flitted between him and Willow. "What's going on?"

"Willow and I were just talking about how much fun she's going to have at camp today because they get to go swimming."

"But I don't want to go," Willow said, fidgeting with the straw in her cup.

"Can you tell us why?" Tate smoothed her curls off her forehead. "Maybe we can help if we know what's bothering you."

"I only like the pool when you and Mommy are with me. Not strangers."

Eliana sat on the edge of the sofa and clasped her hands in her lap. "The camp director said there would be plenty of lifeguards. You'll be safe in the pool."

Willow flipped the cover of her book open and closed. "It won't be the same," she whispered.

Man, he was out of his element here. He didn't usually struggle with encouraging Willow to step outside her comfort zone. Probably because she was often the first in line for a new adventure. This morning he couldn't seem to find the right words.

"What if I come inside and watch you swim?" Eliana asked. "There's bleachers, or I can find a chair on the pool deck. I'll stay the whole time, and if you don't feel comfortable in the water, you can get out and sit with me. How does that sound?"

Willow nodded. "Sounds good."

"Great idea." Tate pushed to his feet. "Thank you."

"You're welcome." The purple hue under her eyes left him feeling unsettled. Had she lost sleep over their kiss, too?

"What else can I do to help? Where's Hunter?"

"Still sleeping." Tate reached out a hand toward Willow. "Sweet pea, it's time for you to go get dressed. I'll get Hunter in a minute. Eliana and I need to talk."

She raised one eyebrow. "We do?"

Willow let him gently pull her up off the floor, then she scampered down the hallway toward the bedroom.

"Yes, we do. What happened with my parents? What did they say?"

He'd wanted to lead with a conversation about the kiss, but he wasn't quite that brave—not with the kids around. "Thank you for offering to stay at camp, by the way. You didn't have to do that."

"You looked kind of desperate for a workable solution. It was the first thing that came to mind." She stood and scooted past him, then stopped to examine the backpacks slouched on the floor behind the sofa. "Are their backpacks packed with snacks, lunch, water...all the things?"

"Eliana, please. Tell me what my parents said."

"They tried to persuade the council members and Mayor Lovell that the café wasn't worth repairing. I argued that it was and that the people of Hearts Bay should get to discuss the zoning change."

"Wow, that's great. I'm glad you spoke up." He wanted to hug her, but the way she wrapped her arms around her torso and rubbed her palms against the sleeves of her mint-green T-shirt gave him definitive *stay back* vibes. Worse, her stricken expression confused him. "Isn't it great? That's what you wanted, right?"

His parents had seemed downright hostile to the idea of Eliana keeping the café open. He was proud of her for advocating for herself and others. So why was she acting so distraught?

She strode toward the kitchen. He followed her. She grabbed the scrambled egg skillet off the stove and put it in the sink.

"Eliana, talk to me." He leaned against the counter beside the sink. "What's wrong?"

She squirted dish soap into the skillet and turned on the water. "I'm not sure this is what I want anymore."

Her words landed like a hammer on his thumb. "Y-you don't want the café?"

She turned off the water and faced him. "I shouldn't have kissed you. I'm sorry. I know I crossed the line. It was a stupid, impulsive move and—"

"I didn't think it was stupid. Thought it was amazing, actually."

"This isn't funny."

"I'm not making a joke." He tucked his hands in the back pockets of his jeans to keep from reaching for her. "That kiss was incredible. You have nothing to be sorry about."

Was now a good time to mention he'd thought about that kiss a dozen times already? That right this minute he wanted to cup her cheek in his palm and recreate the moment?

The tightness in her jaw as she stared him down indicated he probably shouldn't go there. At least not right now.

"This is coming out all wrong." She groaned, opening the dishwasher, then loaded his breakfast dishes inside. "We need to go back to being friends. *Just* friends. Two people who have a short-term agreement. I appreciate your efforts to change your parents' perspective, but it's out of our hands now. I'll still take care of the twins. I heard about Christian's new job, and I know you'll have to fish more. Don't worry, I won't back out on our agreement. When the summer's over, you'll go back to Boise and I'll find a new job here if I need to. Or maybe I'll go back to school and start a new career."

The smile she flashed him over her shoulder scraped

his heart raw. *No, not just friends*, he wanted to protest. Because he couldn't fathom going back to Boise without her. He adjusted the brim on his baseball cap. Bare feet slapping against the floor saved him from having to answer. Hunter bounded into the kitchen and slammed into Tate's legs.

"I'm hungry and I have to use the bathroom," he said, dancing around in front of the refrigerator.

"Why don't you start with the restroom, buddy? I'll get you breakfast. Don't forget to wash your hands."

Eliana closed the dishwasher door. "You didn't answer. Are we friends?"

"Absolutely." He brushed past her to get the cereal in the pantry so he didn't have to make eye contact. "Thanks for agreeing to keep watching the twins. They really like you."

"Good. I'll get them to camp."

He pulled a box of Hunter's favorite cereal from the shelf. Too many questions spooled in his head. Had she infuriated his parents by challenging the zoning change? Were they so confident they'd get what they wanted that this morning's meeting was just for optics? If the zoning didn't change, were they still willing to sell; but just not to a Madden?

And why had she reduced their relationship to a business transaction?

That part hurt the most, especially after the kiss they'd shared.

But what could he say? He wasn't about to beg for a relationship. Or stand in the way of her dreams, especially if she wanted to pursue a new career. If their families were ever going to end the festering conflict, maybe the change started here. Now. He'd show Eliana that he'd changed. That he wasn't the selfish guy who'd left her behind all those years ago.

"I'm proud of you." Eliana opened the door of the Trading Post and ushered the twins inside. "You are both so brave."

"I went off the diving board," Hunter said. "All by myself."

Willow scoffed. "With your floaty on."

His proud smile vanished. "Doesn't matter. Floaties still count."

"Willow, I saw you put your face in the water and swim from one side of the pool to the other. That was awesome." Eliana led them to the counter. "We'll eat the lunches your dad packed, but let's order special drinks and a treat to celebrate a great day at camp."

"And for being brave." Willow poked her finger in the air. "Don't forget that part."

"Right."

The hiss of the steam wand frothing milk drowned out their conversation. Annie waved from behind the espresso machine. "I'll be with you in a sec."

Eliana smiled at her best friend, then surveyed the dining area. "Willow and Hunter, why don't you go put your water bottles and lunch boxes on one of those open tables while I stand in line?"

They walked quickly to one of the square tables near the window. Eliana didn't take her eyes off them. As they circled the chairs several times, she almost intervened, certain an argument was about to erupt. Then they plunked their water bottles and lunch bags on the table and hurried back to her side.

"Great choice. That table is my favorite, too." She

patted them both on the shoulder and steered them back into the line. Hunter yawned, then rubbed his eyes. Willow sagged against her leg. Uh-oh. Maybe a lunch outing was a poor decision after a busy morning. She still hadn't figured out when to encourage more activity and when they'd had enough. Hunter and Willow were so articulate, sometimes Eliana forgot they weren't quite five years old yet.

Annie delivered the drink she'd made for the customer waiting at the other end of the counter, then returned to her post between the register and the espresso machine. "What can I get you?"

"I have two very brave swimmers here," Eliana said. "They get to pick a drink and a special treat. We're celebrating a wonderful day at camp."

Annie's green eyes rounded. "That's awesome. Great job, kiddos. We love celebrating bravery around here. We have juice boxes, chocolate milk, regular milk, lemonade, Italian sodas…"

They both ordered chocolate milk, then pressed their faces to the glass bakery case housing the scrumptious treats.

Eliana opened her mouth to correct them about leaving fingerprints and smudges on the glass, but Annie silently implored her to let it go.

All right. Fine. They were celebrating bravery, not perfect behavior. She pressed her lips tight.

"May I have a chocolate chip cookie? A big one?" Hunter pointed to the cookies on a pedestal, which had to be larger than one of his palms.

"Of course." Annie slid the door open. "And for you, Miss Willow?"

"A cake pop, please. The pink one."

"Coming right up," Annie said. "My, your manners are incredible. Thank you for being so polite."

The twins beamed up at Eliana. She patted their heads. "So many wonderful things to celebrate today, right?"

"What can I get you, Eliana?"

"May I please have a mixed-berry smoothie?"

"Absolutely." Annie took Eliana's debit card and swiped it. "I'll bring this all out to you in a few minutes."

"Thank you."

Eliana and the twins sat down at the table. She helped open their lunch boxes and get out their sandwiches. The weight of curious stares warmed her skin as she claimed the seat beside Hunter. She made direct eye contact with Mrs. Lovell, the mayor's wife, who was sitting at the next table, and offered a friendly smile. No doubt people were already talking about Tate, his kids and the café's future. Sitting here with Willow and Hunter would fuel more speculation. She refused to let that bother her, though. There was nothing wrong with helping a friend who needed reliable childcare. Even a friend she'd enjoyed kissing just a little too much.

She fished a banana and a protein bar out of her purse. Hunter wrinkled his nose. "That's your lunch?"

"This, plus the smoothie Miss Annie's going to bring me. What are you having?"

"Sandwich, chips and fruit. Plus the yummy treats that Miss Annie is going to bring *me*."

He emphasized the last word with a big smile and leaned toward her, bumping his shoulder against hers. She smiled and peeled her banana. He was so adorable. She couldn't possibly admit that her conversation with their father was the reason why her stomach was still tied in knots. Little kids didn't need to know that stuff.

She'd crushed Tate with her words and didn't know what to do to make it right.

She had meant what she'd said. Sort of. That kiss had crossed the line. Shoved their friendship into the romantic-relationship zone. But forgetting how his kiss made her feel would be like asking a fisherman to forget how to fish. And judging by Tate's reaction in the kitchen this morning, he felt the same way.

Annie carried their drinks and desserts over on a brown vinyl tray. "Here you go. Two chocolate milks and one mixed-berry smoothie." She set the drinks down, then added the cake pop and chocolate chip cookie to the middle of the table. The kids clapped their hands.

"Can I get you anything else?"

"No, thank you," Eliana said.

Annie's smile faded. "Are you sure? Maybe a pep talk or a heart-to-heart?"

Eliana paused, her banana halfway to her mouth. Her conflicted feelings were that obvious?

"Yes, your feelings are written all over your face. You forget we've been friends our entire lives. I know all of your looks." She picked up the tray and tucked it under her arm. "Text me when you're ready to talk."

Um, that would be never. Eliana nodded and reached for her smoothie.

The door to the shop opened again, and Eliana's sister Rylee stepped inside. She grinned, then worked her way through the tables.

"Mind if I join you?" She pulled out the other chair beside Willow, hesitating as both the kids stared her down.

"Hey, Rylee. Sure, grab a seat. Hunter and Willow, have you met my sister Rylee yet?"

Willow took a bite of her cake pop and pretended to

ignore the question. She was all about finishing that treat. Eliana couldn't blame her. It looked delicious.

Hunter kicked his sneakers against the chair legs. "I'm Hunter."

"Nice to meet you, Hunter and Willow. Those desserts sure look good. Can I have some?"

Hunter peered at Eliana, probably trying to confirm if Rylee's request had to be acknowledged. What a sweetie. He didn't want to say no, but he didn't want to share, either.

Willow shook her head. "No way."

Well, so much for being polite.

Rylee laughed. "No worries, girlfriend. I'll get my own coffee in a minute." She slipped out of her jacket with the Hearts Bay Aviation logo stitched on the front, then draped her purse strap over the back of the chair.

"No flights this afternoon?" Eliana pulled some extra napkins from the dispenser and set them on the table between the twins.

"I had two sightseeing tours back-to-back this morning, so now I'm finished for the day. I wanted to stop by and grab Mom some of her favorite tea and a scone. She's having a rough day."

"What do you mean?"

"Have you not heard?" Rylee's phone rang from inside her purse, but she ignored it. "She got dizzy in the shower this morning, then slipped and fell."

The last bite of her protein bar turned to cardboard in her mouth. "Why didn't anyone tell me?"

"Maybe Dad was waiting until he had more information." Rylee grabbed her phone, glanced at the screen, then dropped it back in her purse.

"But how did you find out?" Eliana didn't want to

sound like a brat, but it hurt her feelings that she might've been the last to know about Mom's incident.

"Tess told me." Rylee slid the hair tie from her wrist and pulled her long, dark hair into a ponytail. "When I hear more details, I'll be sure to share. As far as I know, she's resting at home."

"Can I have another drink, please?" Hunter smiled sweetly at Eliana. He had scattered chocolate chip cookie crumbs all over the table and had a smudge of mayonnaise from his sandwich on his cheek. Wow, what a mess.

"We'd better stick with water. You've had enough sugar for one afternoon." Eliana pointed to his water bottle. "Finish what you have, and if you're still thirsty, we'll ask Miss Annie for a refill."

Her stomach turned queasy. Mom's health issues were getting more serious, and she'd been too preoccupied with a waterfront zoning ordinance to notice. She pushed her smoothie aside and half listened to the twins chatting with Rylee while they finished their treats. For all her posturing about regretting that kiss, and the praise she'd dished out today for her brave young swimmers, a very real fear had slunk in the back door of her heart. Her comfortable existence was being challenged. And she didn't like it. At all. How could she possibly consider leaving the island for a radiology technician career now? What if her mom needed her?

Chapter Eight

If Eliana wanted to be friends, then he'd accept it. Even if it meant crushing his hopes for the future. A future he'd hoped might include her.

Tate dried his wet hands on his jeans, then crossed the boat deck and turned off the water spigot. His muscles ached, but he'd been determined to finish cleaning the boat after a successful fishing charter. Their clients, four guys from California who'd been friends their whole lives, had all caught plenty of salmon. It had been a long, fun day. The men would go home happy, with great stories to tell for years. He had forgotten how much tourists enjoyed catching fish, admiring the scenery and hearing his dad's stories about life on Orca Island.

If only the day on the water had soothed his heartache.

Eliana had shredded him. And he still couldn't believe his parents were pursuing the zoning change. Somehow he'd hoped that they'd back off when the deal fell through.

"Tate, I'm going to head home." Dad emerged from the boat's cabin. "See you tomorrow."

"See you tomorrow." Tate waved at his father's retreating form. He had so many questions but lacked the energy to have the same old conversation.

He checked the time on his phone. It was just after five. He needed to get upstairs to the apartment so Eliana could go home. Their conversation in the kitchen this morning replayed in his head for at least the fifth time. Yeah, he wanted to see her and the kids and hear about their day at camp, but he was still feeling wounded. How was he supposed to pretend like he wasn't?

He walked around the boat and cleaned up an empty soda can, a water bottle and snack wrappers left behind under one of the bench seats. He stuffed them in an empty plastic shopping bag that doubled as his temporary trash can. The harbor's familiar scents—freshly caught fish and tangy salt water—hung in the air. He paused and admired the clear evening sky, sunlight slanting toward the buildings lining the waterfront and vibrant flowers blooming in planters near the sidewalk. This place was spectacular. Idaho had a beauty all its own, but nothing beat Orca Island on a sunny summer day.

If his parents sold their property and the boat, closed their businesses, and retired out of state, he'd be so disappointed. Not that he wouldn't come back to visit Christian, Sarah and their little one, but it wouldn't be the same if his parents didn't live here anymore.

He lifted his ball cap and scratched his head. This train of thought only put him in a bad mood. Because if he didn't visit Hearts Bay, then he wouldn't see Eliana, either. His chest pinched. The twins really liked her. *He* really liked her. Not that he wanted to keep Jade and the kids separated for much longer. Sure, she had plenty of shortcomings, but she was also their mother, and Willow and Hunter needed her. Jade's new husband, Chad, was a professional musician with the Boise symphony, so there was no way they'd ever consider moving to Alaska. That thought made him smile. Jade would hate it here.

Have you asked Eliana to come to Boise?

Tate jammed his hat back in place and barked out a laugh. Man, the voice of reason could really be irritating sometimes. No, he hadn't asked Eliana to come to Boise. Because she'd declared that kiss was a mistake. So why put himself in a situation where she'd reject him again?

But the idea had taken root. Sinking down into his soul and digging in, like Willow when she refused to obey. What was so wrong about imagining a future that included her, the twins, Jade and Chad all in the same zip code?

"Because it's never going to happen," he growled. With the bag of trash dangling from his hand, he closed and locked the boat's cabin door. He crossed the deck, climbed onto the dock, then hurried toward the ramp leading up to the street. Stopping at the dumpster to deposit the trash, his thoughts returned to Eliana. She wanted to be friends. He wanted something more.

But he couldn't possibly ask her to move to Boise. Could he?

His boots thumped on the wooden stairs as he slowly made his way to the top. They'd kissed *one* time. And even though he very much wanted to kiss her again, she wasn't okay with that. He hadn't asked her about whom she'd dated or if she even wanted to get married, but she wasn't behaving like she longed for a serious commitment.

Besides, he'd been selfish once before, and his choices had caused Eliana pain. He wouldn't allow himself to behave that way again. Asking her to change her plans for him sounded pretty stinking selfish.

"Daddy's home!" Hunter yelled the instant Tate stepped inside the apartment. He barely had the door closed before his son was barreling toward him. Willow wasn't far behind.

"Daddy, we swimmed today, and I jumped off the diving board all by myself."

"And I put my face in the water."

"We had chocolate milk and a cookie and now I want pizza." Hunter wrapped his arms around Tate's leg and grinned up at him. "Do you want pizza?"

"I had a cake pop. It was so good." Willow clung to his other leg. "Can we get pizza? Let's go out. I don't want to order it here. I want—"

"Whoa." Tate held up both of his hands. "Take a breath, people."

He took slow, exaggerated steps across the entryway, pretending to drag them across the floor. They giggled and tightened their grip. Hunter would climb all the way up to his shoulders if Tate would let him.

"Welcome to the party." Eliana leaned against the archway to the kitchen, her closed-off expression threatening to smother his attempt to keep things lighthearted. Effortless. As if she hadn't wounded him with her rejection.

"All right, my little monkeys." He managed to extract himself from their hold. "I thought I heard something about pizza."

"I didn't see anything frozen in the freezer," Eliana said. "I told them we should wait and see what you wanted."

"Pizza, pizza, we want pizza." The kids started hopping up and down and chanting.

Tate tore his gaze away from Eliana. "All right, all right. Give me ten minutes to take a shower, and then we'll head over to Maverick's. I hope you're coming with us." He flashed Eliana his most casual grin as he paused beside her on his way down the hall. "I have a reputation as the unofficial Ping-Pong champion to uphold. It would be a shame if you passed on your opportunity to knock me off the leaderboard."

Okay, so that was cheesy, appealing to her competitive nature to get her to have dinner with them. But at this point, he wasn't above a little innocent manipulation.

She folded her arms across the front of the Adventure Awaits logo on her teal-green T-shirt. A muscle in her jaw twitched.

Gotcha. He arched a brow. "Well? Are you in or out?"

That familiar spark flashed in her eyes. "Challenge accepted."

Yes! He punched the air with his fist. He hadn't been to the restaurant in years. Hopefully, the owner had kept the Ping-Pong table. And left Tate's name on the so-called wall of fame. Ping-Pong wasn't a game Jade relished, so Tate hadn't played since college. But that didn't matter. This was one more way to spend time with Eliana. Even if he embarrassed himself, he'd still call the evening a win because they'd spent it together.

A man shouldn't look that good playing Ping-Pong.

The scuffed plastic ball bounced on the edge of the table and sailed past her.

"I win." Tate dropped his paddle on the table and

thrust both arms in the air. "Want to play best out of seven?"

"Hmm, tempting, but no." Eliana shot him a glare. Although another game meant more time to admire the way that royal blue T-shirt emphasized the blue in his eyes. No. She gave the idea a mental push. Her ego couldn't take another shellacking. She had won the first game. Barely. Then he'd won three straight.

He smirked. "You really hate losing, don't you?"

Those entirely too-kissable lips infuriated her.

She turned away and pretended to look for the Ping-Pong ball that had rolled out of sight. Maybe they should play darts instead. There was something so satisfying about hitting that bull's-eye. But she hadn't thrown darts in ages, and he'd probably beat her at that, too.

She retrieved the ball from under a stool and returned it to the table along with her paddle. Tate had crossed from his side to hers. Propping his hip against the table, he linked his arms over his chest. Her eyes drifted to the short sleeves on his T-shirt, hugging his biceps like it was their job.

He caught her staring. There was that aggravating smirk again.

Blood rushed to her cheeks. "I need a soda. Don't you need to check on your kids or something?"

Tate craned his neck and looked past her. "I can see them. Everything's fine. Still having a ball out there."

The owner of Maverick's had fenced in the back lot and added a small kids' play area and a new trampoline. This place had long been a favorite of locals, especially the families living nearby in coast guard housing. It offered frequent weeknight specials, including the kids-eat-free option. Judging by the number of families seated inside the restaurant and the kids spilling out into the play area, it was a popular promotion. A breeze blew in through the back door someone had propped open with a cinder block, carrying the sounds of squeals and laughter. Eliana recognized Willow's and Hunter's familiar voices.

"I'll check on them in a minute. First I want to make sure that everything's still okay over here."

"Over where?"

He pushed off from the table and brushed past her, letting his arm graze hers. The warmth of his skin against hers sent a tingle zipping up her shoulder, then all the way to her toes.

Tate made a production out of blowing the dust off a framed picture hanging on the wall. She bit back a laugh as he buffed the glass with the hem of his shirt. A small sign hung nearby, featuring his name as the winner of a tournament during their senior year in high school.

"Oh, please." She groaned. "You're ridiculous."

"What can I say?" He put the picture back, then moved toward her, his eyes locked on hers. He stopped a few inches away. The appealing scent of his aftershave enveloped her. He reached out and let his fingertips skim up her arm. "Some things aren't meant to be forgotten."

Goose bumps danced across her neck and shoulders. "I think I'd better go get that soda." She could barely squeak out the words. What was he *doing*?

And why was it so hot in here? She plucked at the fabric on her T-shirt several times, hoping to circulate some air across her flaming skin.

Annie and Zeke, the guy she'd met at the ribbon-cutting ceremony, had claimed a table nearby. Eliana was one hundred percent certain they'd enjoyed watching that whole conversation go down.

"Here." Zeke vacated his stool. "Sit and catch up. I'll hang with your...friend."

"Thank you." Eliana retrieved her diet soda from the table where she'd eaten dinner with the kids and Tate, then sat down at the high-top across from Annie.

"Having a good time?"

The amusement swimming in Annie's green eyes made her squirm. "Yes. No. I— It's complicated."

Annie swiveled on her stool and glanced toward the Ping-Pong table, where Zeke and Tate were shaking hands. Eliana pulled a long sip of her diet soda through the straw, draining the remainder. Sweet carbonation danced on her tongue, then coated her parched throat.

Annie drummed her fingertips on the table. "Tate's quite friendly tonight."

Eliana grimaced. So they *had* noticed. Super. "We almost kissed. Again."

Annie whipped around, her mouth hanging open.

"Oops." Eliana slapped her palm over her eyes. "Did I say that out loud?"

"Sure did. Now I need details. All of them."

Her memory bombarded her with the details of Tate leaning in, his head tilted, their attraction almost palpable inside the truck's cab. The butterflies in her tummy, undoubtedly rousted from their slumber by Tate's ridiculous flirting, took flight.

"It was a mistake." She rattled the ice in her glass. "That's really all you need to know."

Her flippant dismissal didn't fool Annie. Or subdue the butterflies. Tate caught her watching him, and a slow grin stretched across his face.

Ugh. She pressed her hand to her abdomen, as if that could somehow squelch that silly, fluttery sensation.

"Are you sure you aren't interested in exploring the possibility of a relationship?" Annie leaned across the table. Her green eyes filled with empathy. "I know you really liked him in high school. Tate seems like he's matured into a great guy. I watched you with his kids. They adore you."

"We're growing on each other," Eliana admitted. "But I'm their summer babysitter. In a few weeks, they'll go back to their life in Boise, and I'll be left here to…" She used her straw to jab at the ice in the bottom of her glass, unable to finish the sentence. Left here to what? Lick her wounds? Find a new job and try not to think about how empty her life felt without Tate and the twins?

"Maybe you need a change of scenery." Annie twisted her straw wrapper around her fingers. "I hear Boise is a wonderful place to live."

"I'm not interested in moving to Idaho."

"Not interested or too afraid?"

Whoa. Annie's question stung like lemon juice in a paper cut. Was she really that transparent? Mom probably didn't want people knowing about her health issues yet, so Eliana didn't mention it to Annie. The uncertainty of all that was weighing on her, though.

"Tate isn't the first guy you've fallen for who had plans to live elsewhere." Annie abandoned the paper wrapper and reached for her drink. "I'd hate for location to be the excuse that keeps you from your happily-ever-after."

Eliana tapped her finger against her lip, pondering Annie's advice. She wasn't wrong. A guy stationed on the island with the coast guard had showed up at the café and wooed her with his witty banter and megawatt smile. They'd dated for several months. He'd asked her to consider going with him when he transferred to California, then patiently waited for her to make a decision. Then her brother passed away, and she'd used her grief as a reason to say no. But she didn't miss him the way she was certain she'd miss Tate when he left.

Yeah, so maybe that realization did scare her a little.

Dave, the manager of the restaurant, brought Annie and Zeke's order of chicken wings to the table. "Here you go, ladies. I apologize for the delay. We're swamped tonight."

"No problem." Annie moved Zeke's soda aside. "The wings are worth the wait."

"Happy to hear that." The corners of his eyes crinkled as he grinned and set the platter and a stack of white plates on the table. "Eliana, it's good to see you. Sorry to hear about the damage to the café. Any plans to reopen?"

"Not yet." She tried to keep her tone lighthearted. "When we have a grand reopening date, you'll be among the first to know."

"Right on." Dave smoothed his palm over his bald head. He'd always been kind and encouraging. He was about ten years older than she and Annie and had grown up in Hearts Bay. As a small-business owner on the island, he often shared marketing tips and helped troubleshoot issues whenever he'd stopped by the café.

"I hope you're going to speak at the town council meeting tomorrow night." His expression grew serious. "I'm assuming you're not in favor of changing the zoning for the waterfront."

She tucked a strand of hair behind her ear. "I'm not in favor of the change, but I've shared my opinion already, and I feel like Rex and Tammy have this one locked down."

"Sadly, I'm afraid you might be right." Dave's dark eyes narrowed. He cast a suspicious glance at the tables nearby, then leaned closer. "Rex and Tammy have been in here with at least three of the council members. Buying them dinner, bending their ear—you get the picture. I heard the deal Rex had on the table fell through, but there will be another one before too long. They might already have other developers waiting to make offers. If Rex gets his way, there's no stopping him from selling both those lots. Then that waterfront will never be the same. We need you to speak up."

"No pressure or anything," Annie said.

The pizza Eliana had eaten for dinner congealed in her tummy. "Thanks for the heads-up. I'll be there."

"Good. Be sure to stop by town hall or call over there tomorrow and get your name on the list to speak. There will be plenty of people who want to step up to the mic, and I'd hate for you to miss your opportunity." He patted her shoulder. "Don't worry, we're on your side. Have a good night."

He moved on to the next table and stopped to speak to the customers sitting there.

"I'm going to go." Eliana climbed down from the stool. "Please thank Zeke for letting me barge in on your date."

"You can stay." Annie's brow furrowed. "Zeke and I don't mind."

"No, I—I'm tired. I need to go. Dave's right. I've got some prep work to do. Talk to you soon."

She grabbed her purse, plucked her keys from inside and hurried toward the door. She said good-night to the hostess by the front door and stepped outside.

The council meeting to discuss the zoning change was happening much sooner than she'd expected. Originally it was supposed to be a week from now. Dave's news that Rex and Tammy were working hard to influence the vote made her blood boil.

She kicked at a pebble in her path. Rex Adams was so slimy. Had that early-morning meeting with the council members been staged? A phony public display of fairness, while Rex and Tammy had been working behind the scenes to make sure they got what they wanted? She sidestepped a group of people walking toward the front of Maverick's, then quickened her steps. If she hurried to her car, she could leave before Tate noticed.

Rounding the building, she caught sight of him standing inside the fence near the trampoline. No.

"Eliana, hold up." He gripped the top of the fence with both hands. "Why are you leaving?"

"Have a good night, Tate. Thank you for dinner." The backs of her eyes burned. She was such an idiot for not seeing their underhanded ways. Checking for traffic, she avoided eye contact, then started to cross the street toward the lot where she'd parked.

"Did something happen? What did Dave say to you?"

She groaned and turned to face him. Walking back toward the fence, she stopped inches away. Oh, this was awkward. Willow and Hunter had switched from the trampoline to chasing each other around the plastic slides.

Tate's eyes searched her face. "What's wrong?"

"The town council meeting's been moved up. It's scheduled for tomorrow night, and supposedly your parents have been eating dinner here with council members, trying to sway the vote for a zoning change."

"You're kidding." Anger darkened his eyes. "That's awful."

Was he genuinely surprised? She bit back the snarky question, hating that he was caught in the middle of an impossible situation. "I'm going to go home and work on my speech."

"Do you want any help?"

"Spoiler alert, Tate—our families have been fighting about this for decades. Your parents would not be pleased that you're helping me thwart their plans."

"I'm tired of letting my parents influence my decisions."

Did he really mean that? They stood there for what seemed like an eternity, staring each other down. She wanted to believe that he could help her write a compelling speech. But doubt nagged her, and she questioned his sincerity.

"Thanks, but I need to handle this on my own."

A muscle in his jaw flexed. "Whatever happens at that meeting tomorrow, please remember I'm not my father, Eliana, and I'm on your side."

"Right. Of course. Thanks again for dinner." She forced the words past the lump expanding in her throat. Turning away, she broke into a jog and hurried to her car, letting the tears fall. She had to give Rex and Tammy credit—they'd stop at nothing to advocate for their future. Even if it meant stomping all over hers. And as much as she wanted to believe that Tate's comments were genuine, she feared she'd let her feelings for him—and that incredible kiss—cloud her judgment.

She choked back a sob. *You're so naive. When will you learn that an Adams can't be trusted?*

Chapter Nine

❧

Tate's sneakers slapped against the linoleum floors inside the town hall as he jogged down the corridor toward the conference room. The clock mounted on the wall beside the darkened window of the administrative assistant's office taunted him. He was late. Two teenage girls who worked at the twins' day camp had agreed to babysit tonight, but they'd showed up at six thirty instead of six.

Willow and Hunter had fallen apart when he'd reminded him that he had to go out for the evening, but they'd calmed down once the girls distracted them with a board game. He'd made a quick exit from the apartment, although guilt dogged him during his drive over to town hall.

Short of a natural disaster or another emergency with the kids, he refused to miss this meeting. Not after the conversation he'd had with Eliana outside Maverick's last night. He hadn't slept well, knowing she was hurting and still refused his help. The rumors that his parents had relentlessly campaigned to get what they wanted made him punch his pillow a few times.

Did they really want to retire or did they want to claim their victory in this tired old dispute?

At the end of the hall, he paused outside the double doors and peered through the narrow rectangular window. Council members sat behind long tables at the front, facing the audience. Pressing the lever on the door, he eased it open. The hinges squeaked. Several heads swiveled his direction. He slipped inside and let the door click shut behind him, then scanned the packed room.

Eliana sat with her sisters and parents on the left side, second row from the front, and directly across the aisle from his parents, Christian and Sarah. They hadn't saved him a seat. An ache hollowed his stomach. Not that he agreed with what they were advocating for, but at the same time, his absence in that row felt conspicuous. The curious glances directed his way confirmed his feelings. People were silently questioning his arrival. Was he just late? Or not welcome?

It didn't matter now. He was here and intended to stay until he heard the final vote. Moving away from the door, he wedged his frame into an empty place along the back wall. Some folks standing beside him he recognized as other business owners in the community. In front of him, the overhead light gleamed off a man's bald head—Dave from Maverick's sat in the back row with a pad of paper and a pen balanced on his lap.

The room was hot. Tate shed the plaid button-down that he'd layered over a T-shirt and tied the sleeves around his waist. He accidentally elbowed the guy standing next to him.

"Sorry," Tate whispered.

The man gave him a curt nod, then hooked his thumbs in the belt loops of his stained and faded jeans. An aroma of gasoline or motor oil hung in the air. Perhaps the man owned one of the gas stations in Hearts Bay and wanted to hear how the zoning change might impact the island's economy.

Tate folded his arms across his chest. His limbs tingled. For better or for worse, his parents' actions had a ripple effect throughout the community. And he feared the outcome wasn't going to favor Eliana's plans.

A podium with a microphone had been arranged at the front of the room not far from where Eliana and her family sat. The councilwoman serving as moderator shuffled some papers on the table, then quickly reviewed the procedures for the evening. Tate studied Eliana. He couldn't see her expression from this angle, but her ramrod-straight posture and the subtle lift of her chin indicated that she was stressed. He couldn't see her hands, either, but he knew she probably had them clasped in her lap, with the pad of one thumb rubbing the knuckles of the other. She always did that when she was anxious, too.

He forced himself to focus on the woman speaking. She reiterated that after hearing from community members representing both sides of the issue, the council would vote. A proposed zoning change received full approval when five or more members of the seven-member town council voted yes.

A murmur washed through the crowd. Tate chewed the inside of his cheek. They'd vote tonight? Why had he thought there'd be more discussion? A waiting period or something.

If his parents had manipulated people behind the scenes like Eliana suspected, they probably already had five guaranteed votes in their favor. As much as he wanted to believe that his parents' intentions were good, that all they really wanted was to secure their financial future, he couldn't dismiss Eliana's suspicions.

Spoiler alert, Tate—our families have been fighting about this for decades.

Her words had stung. Even though he wanted no part in his parents' schemes, he understood why Eliana felt slighted. He had to find a way to demonstrate that he was not on his parents' side. So far his words hadn't been convincing.

The moderator opened the floor for comments and invited a young woman up to the microphone. Tate recognized her name. She was part of a family who'd lived on Orca Island for years. Her photography business had grown exponentially since Hearts Bay became a popular wedding destination. With her blond hair twisted in a neat bun and her conservative blouse and smart trousers, she carried herself with grace and poise. Icy fingers of dread crawled along Tate's spine as she presented a convincing argument for changing the zoning to allow for the construction of a waterfront venue that catered to brides and grooms.

The owner of the florist shop spoke next. She, too, campaigned for a venue that prospective brides and grooms would find more appealing than the local churches and the community center. She must've been friends with Tammy, because she smiled sweetly in his mother's direction more than once.

Movement from the corner of his eye caught his attention. Rylee Madden leaned toward Eliana, gesturing animatedly with her hands while she spoke. Eliana nodded, then settled back in her chair. Tate moved his hand over his jaw. Mom and Dad might think they had this thing locked down, but if he knew Eliana like he thought he did, she'd deliver a compelling speech.

Two men spoke next, both presenting variations of the same argument—that Hearts Bay was the largest community on Orca Island but needed to preserve the tightly knit small-town feeling that residents valued. Tate groaned inwardly when both admitted that the heart-shaped rock had brought much-needed income to the area. People wanted destination weddings, and getting married on an island in Alaska near a heart-shaped rock had created another revenue stream for the town.

Tate shifted from one foot to the other. What happened to people expressing opinions for both sides of the issue? So far this sounded like nothing but support for a convention center. The second gentleman concluded his speech by insisting that the community had always provided adequate space for meetings and special events. Hearts Bay already met the needs of the local residents and the coast guard without a large, modern venue or a luxury hotel. He requested that the council vote no on the zoning change.

Eliana stood as the moderator gave a brief introduction, then invited her to come forward. She looked beautiful. Her long hair cascaded past her shoulders. The hem of her teal-green dress swirled around her bare legs as she strode toward the podium. When she faced the audience, her gorgeous dark eyes swept the room and landed on him. His heart climbed up in his throat, and he rubbed his palms in slow circles against his pant legs.

Lord, please give her courage and the right words to sway the votes.

Maybe it was a foolish prayer, asking the Lord to work in her favor instead of his own family's. But he didn't care. She wanted this so badly. She deserved to have a thriving business in a building that she owned. Changing the zoning laws to accommodate his parents' preferences wasn't fair. And he wouldn't be able to sleep at night if he didn't root for her.

"Good evening, friends, family, council members and concerned citizens of the community. Thank you for being here and taking the time to listen to both sides of this important issue. In case you are unaware, this issue is personal. For decades my family and Rex and Tammy Adams's family have been tangled in a bitter dispute over who the waterfront property belongs to. At this point I don't know if the truth can ever be established, but I believe that peace is possible. There is a compromise buried under all the hurt and lies."

Tate flinched. He'd wanted her to be bold, but that didn't make the truth palatable. She gripped the edge of the podium with one hand and tucked her hair behind her ear with the other. The air in the room crackled with tension.

"This is about more than a zoning change," she said. "This is about concern for the greater good of Hearts Bay. Because Rex and Tammy have devoted more time to courting offers from real estate developers than repairing their damaged building, my coworkers and I have had to scramble to find new jobs. They forced the café to remain closed for the majority of the summer, without any guarantees that their loyal employees will be able to return to work at the business we've kept running for the Adams family all these years."

"That's not entirely accurate." Tammy rose from her seat, jabbing her finger in the air. "Cathy, this isn't the time or the place—"

Voices erupted in the conference room. Cathy, the moderator, leaned into her microphone. "Mrs. Adams, you're interrupting our speaker. Please sit down. Miss Madden has the floor. Folks, I recognize this can be an emotional discussion. Please refrain from commenting, or I will be forced to remove you from the meeting."

Anger simmered in Tate's stomach. Mom had been completely out of line. Dad reached up and grasped her elbow, then gently guided her back into her chair.

Red splotches dotted Eliana's slender neck. She wouldn't look at him, but he willed her to keep going.

"As others have already stated, a luxury hotel and a state-of-the-art convention center would provide more jobs and possibly bring more prospective brides and grooms to our wonderful community. On the surface those all sound like fantastic opportunities for Orca Island and Hearts Bay."

She angled her body toward the council members. "But tonight, I'm asking you to consider the cost. The impact of your decision, not only for restaurants, but for the whole island. Changing zoning regulations to line the pockets of one particular family sets a horrible precedent and breeds more divisiveness. Thank you for your careful consideration."

A wave of applause washed across the room. Tate joined in, clapping loud enough to earn disapproving stares. He even let out an enthusiastic whoop. Eliana folded her notes in half, then reclaimed her seat. Rylee, Mia, Tess and her parents greeted her with hugs and broad smiles. Warmth flooded Tate's chest. He'd never been prouder of her.

She'd failed.
Plucking a handful of stones from the rocky shore-

line at her feet, Eliana funneled them from one palm to the other. Where had she gone wrong? What should she have said to make the town council vote against the zoning change? Standing at that podium tonight and looking at the faces staring back at her, most were people she'd known her whole life. Several she considered regular customers and friends that felt like family. Buoyed by the warmth of Tate's encouraging gaze, she'd abandoned her notes and poured out her heart in that speech. Even when his mother stood and tried to interrupt her, his calming presence at the back of the room had kept her from freaking out.

But it had all been for nothing.

The town council had voted six to one in favor of rezoning.

She chose one of the rust-colored stones with the white flecks in her hand and flung it into the ocean. The soft plop as the stone submerged was so satisfying. Another wave rolled in, and the green-blue water sloshed around the toes of the black rubber boots she'd borrowed from her mother.

She peeked over her shoulder. Through the windows, she saw her parents, Rylee and Mia still gathered around the table. Likely still picking apart tonight's events. Tess's husband, Asher, and their son, Cameron, had brought her out here. Cameron had shown her how to throw the rocks. She'd pretended to be a rookie, exchanging amused glances with Asher. It had been years since she'd stood out here on the edge of the island and flung pebbles into the sea.

Even though Asher and Tess had taken Cameron home for bed, she'd stayed. Wearing a pair of leggings under her dress, her mother's borrowed boots and her father's oversize yellow windbreaker, she probably looked ridiculous. Not that her appearance mattered. Clearly her efforts to impress anyone with her words or her appearance had fallen short.

The cool breeze blowing in off the water and the orange and crimson streaks trailing the sun across the pale blue sky helped soften the blow of tonight's defeat. She hurled more pebbles into the sea one at a time. How had Rex and Tammy won? This was so not fair. The bad guys weren't supposed to triumph.

Were they?

The rumble of an approaching vehicle and the familiar flash of silver among the trees caught her attention.

Tate.

His truck pulling into her parents' driveway made her want to run and hide.

She scowled in the general direction of his vehicle, then picked her way down the shoreline. Cameron had amassed a wonderful collection of rocks. Hopefully he wouldn't mind if she threw a few more. With a grunt, she chucked one of the larger ones into the water. It went farther than any of her other previous attempts. At least she was good at something.

She rolled her shoulder in a slow circle, wincing at the ache. Maybe she should give it a rest. Tate walked across the yard toward her. Her heart drummed in her chest. There was no point in trying to hide now. He'd only intercept her path before she got to the house.

Blowing out a long breath, she sank down on a large piece of driftwood the tide had long ago discarded on the edge of her parents' property. Despair swept over her. More hot tears pricked her eyelids. She battled them back and tucked her knees to her chest, doubly grateful for the leggings she'd swiped from her mother's dresser drawer. The skirt of her dress was spattered with salt water and noticeably damp along the hem. She squeezed the cotton material in her fist. A few droplets splashed on the ash-gray wood.

Soggy black sand squished under Tate's sneakers. "Mind if I join you?"

She lifted one shoulder, then looked away. "Go ahead."

The driftwood shifted under his weight as he sat down beside her. The wind lifted his hair and rippled the fabric of his navy-and-red-plaid button-down. His careful assessment of her warmed her skin. Tension formed a stubborn fist between her shoulder blades. What to say to the son of the people who'd swept her future plans out from underneath her?

"You did a great job tonight."

His voice carried a note of tenderness that she didn't want to admire. She squeezed her eyes shut.

"I was really proud of you."

Whatever. She mentally shook off the compliment. "Your family still got what they wanted. I'm certain your parents are celebrating right now."

Tate was silent. She braced for him to clap back with a snarky dig.

Instead, he reached for her hand. Slowly unclenched her fist. The calluses on his fingertips skimmed across her palm as he laced his fingers through hers. She was torn. Torn between tugging her hand away or sagging against him and weeping.

She recycled her anger, determined to focus on all the ways his family had hurt her, so she wouldn't have to think about the warmth of his touch. Or the tenderness swimming in those glorious blue eyes.

The whisper-soft caress of his lips when they'd kissed.

"I know my apology probably means nothing at this point, but I am truly sorry that it's come to this."

She searched his face. Memorizing the smile lines in his cheeks. The indentations between his brows. "Are you?"

He nodded slowly. The indentations pinched closer. Pain etched his expression. "I wish things were different."

"Yeah, me, too." She allowed herself to squeeze his hand. It wasn't like she'd ever kiss him again. Was it so wrong to find comfort in the safety of his fingers wrapped around hers? Just for a few minutes?

"There's a bright side. Maybe this is an opportunity for you to try something different, or—"

"Or maybe not." She pulled free and buried her hands in the jacket's pockets. "If this is a when-God-closes-one-door-He-opens-a-window speech, save yourself the trouble, because I already heard it from my sisters."

She yearned to put some distance between them. Except her mom's boots were too big and they'd rubbed raw spots on her heels. With the tide coming in, she was running out of real estate to pace.

Tate folded his hands in his lap and looked at the water, like he was patiently waiting for her to wear herself out.

"Where are the twins? Why aren't you at home putting them to bed?"

"Sarah and Christian are with them. I wanted to make sure you're okay."

Oh.

He gently gathered her hair and draped it over her shoulder. A shiver danced down her spine. His fingers massaged the knots in her neck and unwound the tension camped there. A sigh escaped her lips. Gradually, she relaxed. Dropped her defenses. Against her better judgment, she allowed her head to rest on his shoulder.

He stroked her hair. She closed her eyes. Okay, so she still wanted to drop-kick his parents off the island, but this was nice. Letting somebody help her carry her burdens felt good. She didn't feel so alone with Tate beside her.

"I know you're hurting, and it feels like my family has squeezed the life out of your plans, but this doesn't have to be the end of the road for you. Or for us."

Her breath hitched. She lifted her head and stared at him. "What do you mean, *us*?"

He shifted toward her, their knees bumping together. He took both of her hands in his. The circles he traced on her skin with his thumbs made her stomach quiver.

"Come to Boise."

"Are you kidding me right now?" She leaned back. "Why?"

His thumbs grew still. He pulled away and raked his hand through his hair. "Because I want you in my life. You're great with Willow and Hunter. I think we could have a future together."

She pushed to her feet and took three long strides away. What was he asking, exactly? Pinching her thumb and index finger against the bridge of her nose, she turned in a desperate circle. Her chest constricted. She couldn't think. Couldn't breathe. Turning to face him, she gathered her courage. His blue eyes locked on hers. She couldn't let the hurt swimming there keep her from speaking her mind.

"When you left and went to Idaho, then chose Jade instead of me, I was crushed, Tate. *Crushed.*"

"I—I didn't know how you felt about me, Eliana. I mean, I really liked you and I thought maybe the feeling was mutual. But I was too afraid to say anything. I was selfish and stupid. My family convinced me that I shouldn't date a Madden." He stood and moved toward her. "I'm so very sorry. I never should've listened to their advice. Willow and Hunter are the best gifts God has given me, and I'll always be linked to Jade because of our children—there's nothing I can do to change that. But my children's mother doesn't have to keep you and me apart."

Eliana took a step back. "Our issues aren't only about Jade."

"But—"

She held up her hand to stop him. "Let me finish. Your children are wonderful. I've had so much fun with them. Even the hard days have taught me important lessons. But that doesn't mean you and I are right for each other now. You just confessed that you let your parents influence your choices. I'm not sure I'm ready to trust you. I don't know if I *can* trust you."

His gaze turned frigid. "I'm not going to let my parents tell me who I can date, Eliana. Why can't we start over in Boise?"

Boise with Tate.

"It's not that simple. I—I need time to think." She shivered and jammed her hands inside the jacket's pockets. "I'm going inside. You should go home."

Hurt flashed in his eyes. "That's not the enthusiastic response I'd hoped for."

"Your parents just declared victory over my family

and ruined my hopes of ever owning that café. Forgive me if I'm not ready to pack my bags and follow you more than three thousand miles to start over. Never mind that I don't have a job or a place to live or any friends."

"You'd have me. But that's not enough, is it?"

"Tate, that's not—"

"No, I get it. You don't have to say anything else. How insensitive of me to want you in my life." A muscle in his jaw flexed. "Guess I misread this one. My bad."

He turned and walked away, dodging the waves lapping at the shore, then cutting long strides across the yard toward his truck.

She stood there, letting the water wash over the toes of her boots. He got in his truck, started the engine and drove away. Tears slipped down her cheeks. She'd feared what might happen if their friendship morphed into something more. Feared they'd get so caught up in the emotions that they wouldn't see the heartache looming until it was too late. She'd never imagined it would hurt this much when their families' conflicts drove a spike between them, splintering any hope of a future together.

Chapter Ten

Six miserable days later, Tate wove through several groups of young children gathered on the grass in the middle of the high school's track. Willow and Hunter's camp ended today. The finale included an outdoor extravaganza that evidently involved lots of water balloons and screaming, based on the chaos erupting around him.

"Look out."

A camp counselor blew past Tate, a giggling boy brandishing a can of silly string trailing after him.

"Daddy, over here."

Tate turned in the direction of Hunter's voice. "Hey, pal."

Hunter waved. He stood in line behind four other children. They were waiting for…face paint?

Tate groaned.

A woman fell in step beside him. "Don't panic. It's washable."

He formed his mouth into a smile. "Good to know. Thanks."

"You're welcome. See you around." She winked, then waggled her fingers. The bracelets on her wrist jangled.

Her smile lingered too long, so he quickened his steps, not the least bit interested in continuing the conversation. Where were the parents supposed to go to pick up their kids? Had he arrived too early?

Stumbling to avoid two kids running past him with shaving cream smeared on their hands, he regained his footing in time to see Eliana standing by the fence. Staring at her phone.

His stomach plummeted toward his sneakers. Turning away, he scanned the field for any sign of Willow. Maybe a counselor to check in with? He tugged the brim of his ball cap lower. Thankfully, he'd remembered his sunglasses, too. He needed all the help he could get to disguise the dark circles camped under his eyes. Ever since their painful interaction beside that stupid piece of driftwood last week, he'd wandered around in a fog of regret.

They were barely speaking, but Eliana hadn't abandoned her commitment. She'd dutifully showed up every day and picked Willow and Hunter up from camp. His sister-in-law had been placed on bed rest, so he had agreed to work in the fishing charter office when his mother wasn't available. Eliana stayed with the twins until he closed at 5:00 p.m. She wasn't rude, but she wasn't friendly, either. That guarded expression in her eyes when she met him at the apartment every afternoon and handed off the twins hinted that she hadn't warmed to the idea of starting over in Boise.

Her reaction had gutted him. He wanted so badly for her to change her mind.

But he refused to ask her again. This island was her home. Asking her to leave wasn't fair, and part of him couldn't blame her for retreating into the comfort and safety of her family. Especially since his parents had unapologetically moved forward with their plans. They were already entertaining multiple competing offers for the sale of their property.

Turning in a slow circle to find Willow, he spotted her familiar curls and the bright pink-and-purple-striped T-shirt and lime-green shorts she'd picked out to wear this morning. As she crawled through the flap on the entrance of an inflatable castle and tumbled onto the grass, his chest tightened. She sat up and swiped at the tears on her flushed cheeks.

"Hey, Willow." He jogged toward her, but she didn't hear him. Scrambling to her feet, she started running toward Eliana instead.

His steps faltered as a gaggle of preschoolers darted into his path. He watched as Eliana dropped her phone into her purse and ran to meet Willow. She knelt and gently wiped the tears from Willow's cheeks and listened as his daughter shared her troubles. The tenderness in her touch made his knees wobble. What was going to happen when they were back home and Willow needed help? Jade wasn't exactly oozing with empathy when the kids came to her with a problem. How would Willow and Hunter feel when they looked for Eliana and she wasn't there?

The thought was an iron fist slamming into him. He doubled over, resting his hands on his knees. What had he done? Eliana's absence was going to leave a gaping hole in their lives. One he wasn't sure would ever heal.

He straightened and continued walking toward Eliana and Willow. "Willow, is everything okay?"

"Hi, Daddy." Willow drew a deep breath and stared up at him, squinting in the afternoon sun.

"Some children were being unkind," Eliana said without looking at him. She dug around in her purse, then pulled out a small rectangular container. "Willow just needed to take a minute. Right?"

Willow nodded. "Can I have some lip gloss, please?"

Eliana laughed. "Here." She slid the lid back to reveal a pink concoction inside. "It's watermelon. Your favorite."

Willow swiped her finger through the waxy substance, then rubbed it on her lips. "Mmm. Yummy."

Then she ran off without a backward glance. Evidently all was right with the world.

Tate stared as the mysterious concoction vanished back into her handbag. "If that's the thing that rights all wrongs, I'm going to need a twelve-pack."

Eliana's mouth twitched at the corners. "It's watermelon lip gloss. You can find plenty at the drugstore. It tastes like candy. That's why she's into it."

"Uh-huh." Two lousy syllables were all he could muster. Probably should put a note in his phone so he'd remember those crucial details later. But standing there beside Eliana, so close he could see the smattering of freckles on her nose, all he wanted to do was lace his fingers through hers and tell her how much he appreciated the countless ways she'd loved his children well.

The words died on his tongue. She'd brush off the compliment. Or roll her eyes and tell him she'd only done what any babysitter would do. An awkward silence blanketed them. Her phone buzzed, and she pulled it from her purse, then scanned the screen. Tate looked away, surveying the field for Hunter. He was next in line at the face-painting station.

Eliana finished sending her text. "If you're here to pick up the kids, I'm going to run by the Trading Post.

Annie and I are pulling everything together for the twins' birthday party tomorrow. Annie has the candy to stuff inside the—"

"Wait. What?" He lifted his ball cap and scratched his head. "I thought Sarah was helping Annie plan the party."

"She asked me to take over, since she's on bed rest."

Oh. Nice of Sarah and Christian to keep him informed. He tugged his cap back in place. "Anything I need to take care of? I—I didn't realize you'd been asked to help."

There was that businesslike expression again. Colder than an Arctic blast in the dead of January, she was freezing him out. "Annie and I have it covered. You don't need to worry."

Right. That was the problem—he was worried. His family had crushed her dreams, and she had pressed on. Planned a birthday party for the twins and tried to pretend she wasn't dying inside.

She slung her purse strap onto her shoulder. "I'll meet you back at the apartment in an hour or so."

"Yeah. See you." He managed a cheesy wave before she walked away. Dropping to the grass, he rested his elbows on his knees and waited for Willow and Hunter to finish their camp. He felt sick. They shouldn't have come to Hearts Bay for the summer. If they'd stayed in Boise, the twins wouldn't have grown so attached to Eliana, and he wouldn't have put his heart out there. Leaving was going to hurt. He hated that once again his actions had caused so much pain.

"Surprise!"

The woman stood on the lawn, her long, honey-blond hair spilling down her back in perfect spiral curls. She wore black leather leggings and a leopard-print tunic that revealed toned and tanned bare shoulders. With red nail polish on her toes and her stylish open-toed wedges, even her feet looked pretty.

Every conversation at the party skidded to a halt. All eyes swiveled her way.

"Looks like somebody enjoys making an entrance," Annie grumbled.

Eliana's stomach twisted. That had to be Jade.

Tate vacated his seat at the picnic table, his expression ashen. "Willow, Hunter, look who's here."

Hunter gasped. His plastic fork slipped from his hands and landed on the picnic table, scattering bits of chocolate cake across the red vinyl tablecloth.

Jade abandoned her luggage and black designer handbag on the ground and stretched her arms wide.

"Mommy!" Willow jumped up and raced toward her mother, squealing with delight. Hunter scrambled off the picnic table bench.

"Wait for me." He ran after Willow, tripping and stumbling across the grass.

Eliana clutched Annie's arm. Oh, he'd be so embarrassed if he fell in front of everyone. Thankfully, he made it to his mother's side, and she folded him into a hug.

Conversation resumed in fits and starts, rippling around her, but Eliana stood paralyzed, watching the twins' and Jade's reunion. She glanced at Tate. He stood off to Jade's right, hands on his hips, a muscle in his cheek twitching. Eliana let her gaze flit to Tammy and Rex. They hadn't moved from the opposite end of the picnic table. Neither looked thrilled about the party crasher's arrival.

"Come on, help me put more water and soda in the cooler." Annie motioned for Eliana to walk with her.

"What? Now?"

Annie angled her head toward the tables where they'd stashed an extra case of bottled water, juice boxes and soda. "It's warm today—people need plenty to drink."

"This is Alaska, not Palm Springs." The afternoon sun warmed her back as she trailed after Annie. Halfway to the table, she realized Annie's scheme. If they restocked the drinks, they'd be able to hear Jade and Tate's conversation.

Brilliant.

Eliana jogged to catch up. "I like the way you think."

Annie shot her a wink. "Thought you might."

She stopped at the table holding the snacks and remnants of the sheet cake. Most of the kids had finished eating and moved on to climbing on the park's play structure.

"Wow, Jade, this is quite a surprise." Tate's words filtered toward her as she cleaned up stray chips and neglected bits of popcorn from the table. "How did you know the party was here?"

"Willow called me two days ago and gave me most of the details. I asked the taxi driver who picked me up at the airport to drop me off at the park. He knew exactly where to go." Jade laughed. "Got to love a small town, right?"

Eliana stole a glance at Tate. His hardened expression made her wince. Poor guy. Based on the little bits of info he'd shared, Jade's arrival would make his life complicated. She lifted the lid on the cooler, then added more cans of soda and a few more juice boxes.

"You didn't think I'd miss your birthday, did you?"

Jade smoothed her hands over Willow's and Hunter's curls.

Eliana couldn't help but glare. That was Willow's biggest fear. She'd asked for Eliana's help texting Jade several times, though she'd never said why. Eliana had consistently sidestepped the request. Willow got angry when Eliana reminded her that Tate needed to help her with contacting Jade. Now the little girl's frustration made more sense.

"Oh, my. Hunter, *what* are you wearing?" Jade's snide comment paired with her obnoxious laughter sent a bolt of anger zipping straight through Eliana. She'd helped Hunter find his denim cargo shorts and his purple T-shirt with the rocket ship on the front. What was wrong with his outfit? At least the clothes were clean. After he was dressed, he'd flashed her that adorable grin and said the shirt was his favorite. Wasn't his happiness and comfort more important than Jade's opinion?

Hunter's shoulders sagged, and he hung his head, twisting his little hands in the hem of his T-shirt.

"Oh, no," Annie whispered.

"Jade." Tate's stern voice held a warning.

The woman's smile morphed into an irritated frown. "What?"

Tate gave an almost imperceptible shake of his head.

"Oh." Jade's gaze darted toward the party guests. She pasted on a smile, then planted a kiss on Hunter's head. "You know I'm kidding, buddy. You look super handsome. Just like always."

"What about me?" Willow whined.

Jade turned her attention to her little girl. "And you, my dear, look lovely in polka dots. I *adore* that yellow-and-pink combo."

Willow beamed and twirled in a circle.

Annie closed the lid on the cooler, then crossed her arms. "She's really something, isn't she?"

Before Eliana could comment, Jade's gaze met hers. The flawless smile evaporated. Eliana tried not to glare. The woman had every right to show up at her kids' birthday party, even if she did suck the fun right out of the gathering.

Maybe that was Jade's objective.

Eliana turned away and tried to focus on helping a little girl refill her paper plate with apple slices. The brief distraction didn't prevent her from overhearing Willow's conversation with Jade.

"But our camp is closed tomorrow, so we're supposed to hike and pick berries." Willow turned toward Eliana, her worried expression seeking confirmation. "You said you'd take us."

"I'll come by in the morning like I always do," Eliana said, forcing herself to keep her tone upbeat. "Your mom is more than welcome to come with us."

"Berries. Right." Jade's perfect brow furrowed into a valley, as if Eliana had suggested she shovel cow manure for the afternoon. "I'd love to go on a hike."

Sure, you would.

Tate bit back a smile, and it was all Eliana could do not to burst out laughing. "Wonderful. We're leaving at nine o'clock. Meet us in front of the apartment, and don't forget your bug spray."

"Can we open presents now?" Hunter tugged on Tate's hand. "I'm tired of waiting."

"Let's do it." Tate allowed Hunter to pull him over to the folding table and chairs where the twins' new friends and Tate's family had stacked wrapped gifts and cards.

Eliana strode back to the picnic table to get her phone so she could take pictures. Dread pitted her stomach. She had zero interest in spending the morning with Jade. But she wasn't going to be childish and deprive the twins of quality time with their mother. Besides, they'd finish picking berries in less than an hour. The walk to and from the car would take thirty minutes. She could handle two hours with Jade. They were both adults. How bad could it be?

"Why are you here?"

Jade's blue eyes widened. "Our children turned five today, Tate. Why would I miss that?"

They stood in front of the island's most luxurious accommodations, an upscale lodge with commanding views of the mountains across the inlet. He should've known she'd pick the fanciest place on the whole island to stay.

"I'm not saying you shouldn't be here." Tate tried to soften his tone. "You've made it clear that you wanted time alone with Chad, so I'm surprised you came all the way to Alaska without him."

Jade looked away. "Chad is preoccupied with his music. Who knew a cello player had to practice so much?"

Ah. Now they were getting somewhere. Chad's demanding career as a professional musician with the Boise symphony had taken time and attention away from Jade. Now that he had other commitments, she was bored.

Tate pushed his hand through his hair. The breeze kicked up, rustling the leaves in the cottonwood trees edging the lodge's property. It was close to 11:00 p.m. His mother had stayed with the twins after they fell asleep so he could drive Jade to the lodge. He was beyond exhausted and wanted to get home to bed, but he had to know her intentions. "Are you planning to take the twins back home with you?"

She met his gaze again. Surprise flickered across her features. "No, of course not. Is that what you think?"

"I'm never sure what to think with you and your surprises."

"Relax." She flashed him a playful smile.

He wasn't going to fall for her faux-carefree attitude. Not this time. She wanted something. He sensed it, like an animal sensed the weather changing by sniffing the air.

"I'm here to see my kids for their birthday. I'll be gone in a couple of days, and you can get back to your summer of love."

"Wait. What?"

She nudged his shoulder with her hand. "You don't have to pretend. I can see that there's something going on between you and Evelyn."

"Eliana."

"What?"

"Her name is Eliana."

"Whatever." Jade shrugged. "She's obviously into you. Don't worry, I'm not here to take you back."

"Good to know." Tate swallowed back the rest of his snide comments. They were divorced. His personal life was none of her business. He circled around to the back of the truck and retrieved her giant suitcase and carry-on.

"Thank you," she said when he set her luggage at her feet.

"You're welcome." He turned to leave, hesitated, then

turned back. "So you'll meet Eliana and the twins in front of our apartment tomorrow at nine?"

Jade clutched her suitcase handle and offered him a blank stare.

Oh, brother. She'd already forgotten. He scrubbed his hand over his face to stifle his exasperation. "Jade, the kids want you to pick berries with them tomorrow. You said you'd be there."

"Oh, right." She frowned. "Nine is kind of early, but I'll try and make it work."

"I'll text you the address."

"Good night."

Tate waved and slid behind the wheel of his borrowed truck. He did not have a good feeling about tomorrow. Maybe he should make sure Eliana was really going to be okay spending a few hours with Jade and the twins. He grabbed his phone and texted Jade the address, along with another reminder about the time and the insect repellent, then scrolled to Eliana's contact info. He started a message, then deleted it. Sighing, he dropped the phone in the console and started the engine.

It was a short hike to pick berries. She didn't need him interfering with his unsolicited advice.

Tate drove away from the lodge with Jade's comments about Eliana echoing in his head. Summer of love? What was she talking about? And what had she seen in the time they'd all been at the party together?

Nothing. That was what.

Because he hadn't gone anywhere near Eliana—he'd barely even looked at her. They'd all been so stunned by Jade's appearance that there hadn't been time to talk about anything else. Typical Jade. Embarrassed by her impulsive choices and now she was trying to deflect his attention elsewhere.

While Eliana probably wasn't thrilled about spending time with his ex-wife, she wouldn't have offered if she wasn't sincere. He had an all-day fishing charter tomorrow, and he wasn't bailing. He couldn't ask his brother to cover for him. Christian had already started his new job. Besides, Sarah had an ultrasound scheduled and an important appointment with her doctor. His brother didn't need to miss that.

Eliana could handle Jade. He had nothing to worry about.

Chapter Eleven

"Where is my mom?" Hunter kicked a pebble on the sidewalk and sent it skittering into the street.

"I'm sure she'll be here soon." Eliana checked the time on her phone. She wasn't sure at all, to be honest. Jade was almost twenty minutes late to pick berries and hike with her own kids.

"Can you text her?" Willow shook her water bottle then held it up to let the sunlight filter through.

"I could if I had her number." Eliana unzipped her backpack and double-checked that she'd packed bear spray, extra granola bars and plenty of Goldfish crackers. They weren't going to be gone long, but she wanted to have Willow and Hunter's favorite snacks in case they got grumpy.

"You don't have her number?" Hunter stared at her wide-eyed, his lower lip already trembling.

Oh, dear. If the lack of a phone number set him off, imagine what he'd do if Jade didn't show up at all.

"Hunter, listen." Eliana knelt beside him and gently clasped his shoulders. "We are going to have lots of fun today. Your mom is probably just running late. It's going to be all right."

Hunter quirked his lips to one side and studied her. Weighing the validity of her words, probably. He seemed to have a special gift for ferreting out her overly optimistic messages. A skill he'd only improved in their weeks together.

The door of the fishing charter business opened, and they all turned to see Tate's mom stepping outside. She held a phone in her hand and wore a frown.

Uh-oh. Eliana braced for her announcement.

"Bad news, kiddos." Tate's mother walked toward them. "Your mom isn't feeling well. She said to go on without her and she'll see you after lunch."

"No way." Hunter glared at his grandmother. "You're teasing us."

"I wouldn't tease you about something like that, sweetie." Tammy and Eliana exchanged sympathetic glances.

"When you get back, I'll take you to visit her at her hotel." The sleigh bell Eliana had tied to her backpack jangled as she slid the straps over her shoulders.

"We can't hike and pick berries without her," Hunter said, tears clinging to his long eyelashes. "She'll miss us too much."

"We don't want her germs," Willow said. "Sick people are s'posed to stay by themselves."

"Let's do a short hike." Eliana infused her voice with as much enthusiasm as she could muster. "We'll pick plenty of berries to share, and when your mom is feeling better, she can try some."

"Uh-uh." Hunter shook his head. "I don't want to."

"Don't be a baby, Hunter," Willow scolded. "We do stuff without Mom all the time."

Eliana's heart squeezed. Most of the time, navigating Willow and Hunter's opposite personalities had come easily to her. Today she didn't know what to say when one insisted on remaining fiercely loyal to their mother while the other was eager for action and adventure.

"Hunter, your dad and your grandfather are halibut fishing way out in the ocean. Your aunt and uncle have a special doctor's appointment, which means I have to stay here and work in the office," Tammy said. "You'll have to go with Eliana and Willow for a couple of hours, because there's no one else to watch you."

"I can stay here," Hunter said. "I'll be super quiet."

Emotion tightened Eliana's throat. His earnestness was so precious. She hated that something fun had turned into a battle.

"You don't want to miss berry picking." Tammy ruffled his hair. "Eliana knows all the great spots for the biggest raspberries."

"I hate raspberries." Hunter crossed his arms over his red fleece pullover and stomped his sneaker against the pavement.

Willow sighed and pushed her curls out of her face. "Don't be dumb, Hunter. You do like raspberries."

"Do not."

"Do so!"

"Okay, okay." Eliana stepped between them. "Here's what we're going to do. We will hike and pick berries like we planned, then when we're finished, we'll eat lunch and take some chicken noodle soup and crackers to your mom. Sound good?"

"Yep." Willow flashed her brother a victorious smile.

Hunter swiped at his tears with the back of his hand. "Can we take her some ginger ale, too?"

Eliana smiled and ruffled his hair. "Of course."

A few minutes later, she had them loaded into their car seats in the back of her car. Tammy waved from the front steps of the office.

They hadn't even pulled out of the parking lot yet and Willow and Hunter were arguing about who saw the most license plates with bears on them the last time they'd ridden in Eliana's car.

Lord, please help me to be kind and not lose my temper. Or think terrible thoughts about Jade. She turned on the audiobook of a popular children's book series, hoping that might break up the squabble.

Thankfully, it worked, and they enjoyed a peaceful ride a few miles out of town to one of Eliana's favorite berry patches. She'd texted her brother-in-law, Asher, yesterday, and he'd confirmed it was a great trail and one he'd recently visited with Cameron. They'd picked enough berries for Tess to make several jars of raspberry jam.

Eliana parked and waited until the audiobook's current chapter finished before she turned off the engine.

"How do raspberries grow?"

"Can you put raspberries in cake?"

"Do they make raspberry ice cream?"

Eliana patiently answered their questions while she applied insect repellent to their arms and necks, then added the special wristbands to ward off even more mosquitoes. Slipping her sunglasses into place, Eliana handed each child their own small plastic bucket.

"All right, my friends. Let's find some raspberries."

The morning sun spilled golden light through the tree

branches as she led the way down the dirt trail from the parking lot. Willow sang off-key and Hunter begged her to stop until he grabbed a stick and swatted at the tall grass. Something about wandering down a path through the woods with a stick made him forget how much Willow irritated him.

Eliana patted the canister of bear spray tucked in the mesh pocket of her backpack. Without another adult along, she'd have to be hypervigilant about bears.

"Look." Willow pointed. "Are those raspberries?"

Eliana slowed her steps. Up ahead, several bushes full of ripe raspberries lined the trail. "Sure are. Let's stop and pick some."

She showed the twins how to gently remove the berries from the bushes and set them in the bucket without squishing the fragile fruit. Well, she tried, anyway. It wasn't realistic to expect five-year-olds to care about getting a bucket full of raspberries home. Maybe today should be about enjoying nature and trying a new activity. This summer had taught her all about adjusting her expectations.

The terrifying sound of an animal snuffling, and branches crackling as it moved toward them, made the hair on the back of her neck stand up.

Oh, no.

"Eliana?" Hunter's voice trembled.

She followed his finger to the trail behind them. A large brown bear and two cubs emerged from the woods and lumbered toward them.

"That's a big bear," Hunter whispered.

Eliana gulped and tugged both kids toward her. "Let's stay real still and maybe she'll keep walking."

"Are those her babies?" Willow whispered, leaning against Eliana's legs.

"I think so." Eliana's heart thundered. She'd seen plenty of bears in her lifetime on the island, but this was the closest she'd come to a mother and her cubs.

"Pew." Hunter waved his hand in front of his nose. "She stinks."

"Hush." Willow tried to press her palm over his mouth. Hunter squealed and pushed Willow. Her bucket slipped from her hands and landed on the ground. Raspberries dotted the dirt at their feet.

"Whoa, whoa, whoa. No pushing." Eliana tried to rescue Willow as she teetered off balance. Too late. Willow lurched and fell, then burst into tears.

The mama bear's head lolled from side to side. She opened her mouth and growled, revealing a massive pink tongue and two rows of sharp yellow teeth.

"Oh, no." Eliana reached down and tugged Willow to her feet.

"My berries," Willow sobbed.

Then Hunter burst into tears.

Come on, think. Spots peppered her vision as she surveyed the woods for their best escape route. But if they ran and the bear gave chase, that wouldn't end well. Yes, she had her canister of bear spray and the bells tied to her backpack. Both seemed useless at this point.

"My hands hurt," Willow said, holding up her scraped palms. "I tore a hole in my pants, too."

"I know. It's going to be okay." Eliana squeezed their shoulders and tugged them closer. She didn't dare take her eyes off the angry animal. If the mama charged them, they'd have bigger problems than Willow's minor cuts.

Suddenly the bear reared up on her hind legs and

pawed at the air, her long black nails swiping through the air. Panic cut through Eliana, sharp and fierce.

"We have to run," she whispered. "Leave your buckets and do exactly what I say."

Hunter wailed, and the bears moved closer.

Willow drew a deep breath. Her body trembled against Eliana's.

"The bears are angry. We can't stay." Eliana tugged both kids by their T-shirts onto the trail. "You have to run. Come on."

"But I'm not fast," Willow cried.

"I can't run, I'm too scared," Hunter whined.

"I'm scared, too," Eliana said, emotion clogging her throat. But she couldn't let anything happen to these kids. Running was their only option. The pungent scent of fish mixed with garbage wafted in the air as the bears gained on them, propelling Eliana to move faster. Clutching Willow's and Hunter's hands in her own, she fled down the dirt path, deeper into the woods.

"Slow down," Hunter cried, tugging on her hand. "I can't keep up."

"Yes, you can," Eliana yelled, desperate for him to stay upright.

"The bears are chasing us," Willow announced, stumbling as she looked over her shoulder.

"Don't look ba—"

Willow tripped over a tree root and fell again.

The horrific sound of the bear's growls thundered in Eliana's ears.

"No, no, no." Eliana paused long enough to scoop Willow up and wedged the hysterical girl on her hip.

"My foot, my foot." Willow sobbed. "It hurts. Bad."

"We can't stop." Eliana pushed the words out and

pressed on, her heart battering her ribs. "Hunter, stick with me, buddy."

"I'm here." Hunter trotted along beside her. "Don't leave me."

"I won't. Promise." Up ahead, an old log cabin came into view. *Thank You, Lord.*

Sweat coated her skin in a slick sheen. Her arms ached, and her lungs burned. Adrenaline pulsed through her veins as she half ran, half stumbled toward the cabin's front door. The sound of the bears' sniffling and crashing through the brush behind her warned her that she couldn't slow down.

A pair of faded gray antlers hung over the door. She didn't have time to worry about trespassing or what she might find inside. The cabin had clearly been abandoned for years, but at least it offered shelter. Maybe the bears would lose interest and wander away if she and the kids hid inside.

She kicked the door open and sent Hunter in first, then followed with Willow. Too terrified to look back, she slammed the door closed. An overturned wooden chair sat in the middle of the floor, coated in dust. Eliana threw her backpack down and lunged for the chair. Willow and Hunter huddled together, still crying. She dragged the chair across the filthy floor, praying it didn't fall apart in her hands. Grunting, she shoved it under the knob and wedged the door closed.

"There." As she gasped for breath, her wobbly legs gave out and she slid to the floor. "We made it."

She pulled the kids close. Hunter clung to her, still whimpering. Willow refused to be touched. She flopped on the floor and clutched her ankle. Tears slid down her cheeks.

Eliana squeezed her eyes shut. Outside, the muffled sound of branches crackling sent her heart into her throat. The bear could force her way into the cabin if she wanted to.

Please, please go away.

They were safe. Except now she had no idea what to do. "Willow, slide my backpack over here, please."

Willow obeyed.

Eliana unzipped the main compartment and reached inside. She'd call Tammy. Or Asher. Or both. Between the three of them, they'd figure out a strategy for getting out of the cabin and back to the car safely.

Oh, no. She dug around in the bottom of the backpack. Where was her phone? The bells jangled as she dumped the contents onto the floor. A lot of good those did. The bears were not the least bit deterred by the noise. She dug through the snacks and extra water bottles. No phone. Hot tears pricked her eyelids.

How was she going to get these kids home if she couldn't call anyone for help?

"How about one last picture before we go?"

Tate took the phone the guy offered. "No problem."

Their clients, three guys from Minneapolis who'd been friends since college, had each caught halibut today. One of which might be a prize winner. They lined up shoulder to shoulder at the back of the boat and grinned. Tate took several pictures before handing the phone back to its owner. When he moved toward the bow to grab the line, he caught a glimpse of Jade and his mother pacing the dock.

He couldn't shake the ominous feeling sliding over him as he noted Jade's worried expression. The grim line of his mother's mouth amplified his worry. What was going on? Letting his gaze slide past them, he searched the dock and the parking lot for any sign of Eliana and the twins. He checked his watch. It was almost six thirty. They weren't still hiking. Were they?

The boat glided toward the dock, bobbing and swaying with the water churned up by its engine. While the guys joked around and made plans for their evening in town, Tate hopped off the boat and secured the lines.

Mom's tight smile made his scalp prickle. "Did you have a good time?"

The guys regaled her with stories of their escapades onboard. Every muscle in Tate's body ached and fatigue clung to him. He couldn't wait to help them clean their fish and send them on their way. They were nice enough, but the sooner he was finished here, the sooner he could find Eliana. He hadn't been able to shake his concerns about Jade treating Eliana poorly while they hiked with the twins.

"Where are Willow and Hunter?" Tate craned his neck to see past Mom and Jade. "Eliana's supposed to be off by six."

"Come over here where we can talk privately." Mom motioned for him to walk farther down the dock. Tate followed, his blood pounding in his ears.

She and Jade stopped several boat slips away, out of earshot of their customers, and faced him. The scent of Jade's overpowering perfume made his nose itch.

"Eliana and the children are missing." Mom twisted one of the strings from her hoodie around her finger. "They never came back from their hike."

"What do you mean, they're *missing*?" A sour taste

burned the back of his throat. "Have you looked for them?"

"That's the problem." Jade propped her hands on her hips. "We don't know where to look."

"I didn't ask her where she was going, exactly," Mom said. "It's Eliana. She's lived here her whole life. She doesn't need my permission to take the kids berry picking."

"Why didn't you tell me sooner?" Tate fought to keep the irritation from his voice. "We have radios for these types of emergencies."

Mom's chin wobbled. "I'm sorry. I—I just kept thinking she'd come back before you got home."

"She should've told someone where she was going." Jade huffed out a breath. "Or at least have a phone. Who hikes without a cell phone these days?"

"She didn't take her phone?" Tate scrubbed his palm across his face. "That doesn't sound like Eliana."

"We've tried calling," Mom said. "It goes straight to voice mail."

"Why aren't you with them?" Tate glared at Jade. "She did this for you, you know."

"So you want me to be missing in the woods, too?" Jade narrowed her gaze. "Thank you for that."

"Don't play games or shift the blame, Jade." Tate retrieved his phone from his pocket. "She included you in their plans so you could spend some time with your children. The reason why you're here. Remember?"

"Who are you calling?"

"The police. Who else?"

While his dad made sure their clients had their halibut weighed and entered in the annual contest, and then they posed for more pictures by the iconic sign at the entrance to the harbor, Tate strode up and down the dock, calling everyone he could think of and asking if they'd seen Eliana and the twins.

Since she'd been gone for several hours and had young children with her, the dispatcher at the police station agreed it was time to activate search and rescue.

He ended the call and walked back to meet Jade and his mother near the boat.

"The search-and-rescue team will start looking right away. And you're sure this was just a hike to get berries?" Tate looked between his mother and Jade.

"What does that mean? What are you asking?" Jade asked, her voice edged with defensiveness.

"Relax, I'm not accusing you of anything. I'm wondering if she mentioned anything else. Going…" He trailed off then swallowed hard. "I just want to make doubly sure she wasn't taking them out on the water, because that's a completely different kind of search."

Jade's face turned pale, and she pressed her hand to her mouth.

"Willow and Hunter were especially rambunctious this morning. I can't imagine she would've gone far," his mother said. "All she had was a backpack with water and snacks."

"So she's injured or had car trouble, or maybe her cell is dead." Tate paced the dock again. "Can you call Asher Hale? I don't have his number. He gave her some hiking suggestions. Maybe he can help us narrow down the search."

"Of course." Mom took her phone from her pocket. Her hand trembled as she scrolled.

A breeze swept across the harbor. Tate tipped his head back. Gray clouds mottled the evening sky. The weather app on Tate's phone had offered an alert of a storm in the forecast. Adrenaline pulsed in his veins. Rain and wind would only make navigation more difficult.

He'd find them, though. No matter how long it took. Even if he had to mobilize the entire island and hike over downed trees and slog through muddy trails. He wouldn't stop searching until Eliana and his children were safe.

"I'm hungry." Hunter kicked his shoe against the cabin's dirty floor. "Do you have more snacks?"

"I'm sorry, we ate everything I brought." Eliana smoothed her hand over his tangled curls. "Someone will find us soon. I'm sure of it."

Outside the cabin's grimy window, the bright blue sky had turned a cloudy gray. Tree branches swayed in the breeze. *Please, please hold back the rain*, she prayed. The cabin provided enough shelter from the outdoors, but she didn't have any dry wood or a way to start a fire to keep warm. Just the thought of an impending storm delaying their rescue and forcing them to spend the night made her want to cry.

"What if you carry Willow on your back? I'll walk." Hunter stared at her, his hopeful expression tugging at her heart.

"But what if the bears are out there?" Willow voiced the concern filtering through Eliana's head. "We can't run fast."

Eliana heaved a sigh. She wasn't a doctor or a nurse, but Willow had injured her foot or ankle when she fell. When the bears couldn't get inside the cabin, they'd lost interest and gone away. But she didn't know how far. Eliana told stories and silly jokes and fed the kids every snack in her bag. Someone had left some jerky and applesauce cups inside the cabin. There wasn't an expiration date, but she figured eventually they'd all get hungry enough to eat both.

The afternoon had dragged on. They'd managed to stay comfortable inside the cabin. Eliana was too scared to leave in case the bears came back. And it was a long walk to the car, especially with an injured five-year-old who had to be carried. Hunter talked a big game, but she didn't think he'd make it all the way back to the car without getting tired. She leaned her head back against the wall of the cabin. Why had she hiked so far into the woods with little kids?

They'd been having so much fun together. Willow and Hunter had finally stopped bickering. The raspberries were fat and sweet and perfect. She'd wanted to squeeze every last ounce of fun she could out of the day. Make a memory Willow and Hunter wouldn't forget and overshadow their disappointment about their mom standing them up.

Today was memorable, all right. These kids would probably never want to go hiking or pick another berry. Ever.

Hunter slumped against her shoulder. "Can I play a game on your phone?"

"I dropped my phone, remember?"

"Oh." He sighed. "I forgot."

"When can we go?" Willow slumped against Eliana's other shoulder. "My leg really hurts."

"And I'm hungry," Hunter added.

"I know." Eliana swallowed back the fresh wave of panic. "I'm hungry and tired, too."

She must've dropped her phone somewhere on the trail when they ran from the bears. If it was lying on the ground near the cabin and she could retrieve it, she would. But the risk of getting too close to the mama bear and her cubs was too great. Leaving the twins alone in this cabin, even for a few minutes, was unthinkable.

"You carry Willow. I'll walk." Hunter stood and dusted off his hands. She had to admire his ability to stick with his plan. Even if it was too dangerous to pull off.

"I'm afraid we won't make it to the car without the bears finding us." She patted her lap and encouraged him to sit with her. "If Willow has a broken bone, it's best that we stay here and wait for someone to find us."

"But that will take forever," Hunter wailed, then flopped onto her outstretched legs.

Eliana grunted, then gently pulled him up to her lap. For a little guy, he could really land hard. "Your dad is probably home from fishing by now, and your mom and grandma have told him to come look for us."

"And Mom and Grandpa Rex, too," Willow whispered.

"How about Uncle Christian and Aunt Sarah?"

"Oh, yes. I'm sure your aunt and uncle are looking." Eliana pressed her cheek to the top of his head. "The people who love us won't stop searching until they find us."

There was probably a lesson in there somewhere about Jesus and His love for them, but she honestly didn't have the energy for profound teaching right now.

"What about your mom and dad and your sisters?" Hunter asked. "Are they looking?"

Eliana's heart squeezed. She hated that her berry-picking adventures had caused people to worry. "If my family knows we're missing, I'm sure they will help look for us."

"Do you have any brothers?" Hunter asked.

"I did. My brother, Charlie, passed away a few years ago."

Willow and Hunter grew very quiet.

"You mean he died?" Hunter asked in a quiet whisper.

"Yes." Eliana scrambled to find a new, happier topic. This was not the time to discuss death and losing loved ones in terrible accidents. Willow and Hunter were already hungry and stranded. She didn't want them to think about terrifying subjects.

"Are you—"

"Wait." Eliana interrupted Hunter's question. "Listen."

The familiar hum of an all-terrain vehicle engine caught her attention. Another human. She gently maneuvered Hunter off her lap and set him on his feet. "That's a four-wheeler."

"Someone found us?" Willow asked.

"I hope so." Eliana stood, then shoved the chair out of the way and tugged the door open.

Three four-wheelers approached, the pungent odors of gas and exhaust permeating the air.

"We're here! Over here!" She jumped up and down in front of the cabin and waved both arms over her head. Asher, Tate and Christian parked their ATVs in a line and turned off the engines.

"Daddy, you found us." Hunter pushed past Eliana and ran toward his father. Tate leaped off the four-wheeler, dropped to his knees and scooped Hunter into his arms. Hunter's body shook with his sobs. Tate's features crumpled as he cupped Hunter's head in his palm. Eliana blinked back tears. Finally. He'd found them.

* * *

They were safe.

Tate kept replaying those three words in his head as he pressed his thumb against the ATV's throttle and steered them down the trail. Rain pelted his helmet. He squinted and hunched forward, determined not to lose sight of Christian and Asher up ahead. When Eliana had taken the extra helmet and indicated she'd ride with him, he'd almost declined. But Willow and Hunter were already settled in with Christian and Asher, and he couldn't just leave her behind. The wind and driving rain made them all miserable, so he'd let her slide in behind him rather than waste time arguing about it.

The fat wheels hit a rut, jostling them, and Eliana wrapped her arms tighter around his waist. Gritting his teeth, he slowed down and steered the machine around a muddy puddle. On any other occasion, he'd relish the opportunity to be this close to her. They'd spent plenty of hours zipping around the island on four-wheelers with their friends when they were younger. Part of him wanted to savor the feeling of her riding behind him, hanging on as he drove them out of the woods and back toward her car.

Except he was so angry he couldn't speak to her.

He sped up, ducking low to avoid a tree branch hanging over the trail. The fragrances of moss and wet soil filled the air. What was she thinking, taking two little kids berry picking this far from town? They could've picked raspberries from the bushes in the park—a short distance from their apartment and with plenty of people around to keep the bears away.

But no. She had to be adventurous and take them deep into the woods. Without telling anyone where they'd gone. Without an emergency action plan and no way to protect herself or his children from an angry, vicious brown bear. Arguably one of nature's most ferocious creatures.

Thankfully, between the short list of suggestions Asher had given Eliana and a family friend recognizing her vehicle in the parking area, they'd been able to get the four-wheelers out into the woods quickly. Rain slid between the base of his helmet and his jacket's collar, sending a chill zipping down his spine. Or maybe it was the thought of Eliana and the kids spending the night out here alone with nothing to eat or any way to keep warm.

Her vehicle came into view, and he guided the four-wheeler up next to it, then slowed to a stop. He refused to turn off the engine and waited for her to move. She hesitated, then slowly unwound her arms from his waist and slid off the side of the machine.

Asher and Christian sped toward the waiting ambulance.

Eliana squeezed his shoulder to get his attention. His gut clenched. He did not want to talk to her. The risk of saying things he'd only regret later was too great. He looked down at her hand, then met her gaze, wounded and questioning. She let go of him, then unsnapped the helmet and pulled it off. Her dark hair tumbled past her shoulders.

She gestured for him to cut the engine.

He grudgingly obeyed. "I need to go."

"I'm sorry, Tate." Her voice broke. "I never meant for this to happen."

"We'll talk later." He glanced toward the ambulance, almost coming undone at the sight of the emergency technicians hovering over Hunter and Willow.

"Don't do this," she pleaded.

"Do what?"

"Shut me out. It was an accident. A terrible mistake."

"It was a terrible lapse in judgment," he growled. "My children could've been killed because of you."

She flinched. "I am so very sorry. Please, you have to believe me. I—"

He didn't wait for her to finish. He couldn't stand there listening to her empty words. It didn't matter how many times she apologized. Her reckless behavior had almost cost him everything. He cranked the engine and drove off, determined to get to his children before they were whisked away.

Blue and red lights blinked on top of the ambulance's cab, spilling their ominous colors into the misty evening air. The reflectors on the EMTs' jackets glowed silver as they helped transfer Willow and Hunter onto a stretcher. Tate parked his four-wheeler next to Christian's and Asher's. Asher had already jogged toward the truck and trailer parked nearby so they could load the machines and go home.

Tate hopped off and hurried toward the back of the ambulance. Through the open doors, he glimpsed Willow swiping at tears on her cheeks. Hunter sat beside her, patting her arm. The tender moment nearly took him to his knees. These children were a precious gift. He'd do everything he could to make sure nothing like this ever happened again.

He didn't recognize the man or the woman examining his children, but he climbed inside anyway.

"I'm Tate Adams. These are my kids, Hunter and Willow. Is it okay if I ride along?"

"Nice to meet you, Tate." The woman hesitated, her stethoscope in hand. "We're going to check their vitals, wrap them in cozy blankets, then we'll be on our way."

"You can sit there." The male EMT pointed to an empty space opposite the stretcher. "Kids, here are some warm blankets."

Tate sat down. His phone hummed in his jacket pocket. He ignored it and placed his hands on top of Willow's and Hunter's. "I'm so sorry this has happened, but I'm here now, and I'm so glad you're safe."

Willow drew a ragged breath. "I love you, Daddy."

"I love you, too," Tate said, swallowing back more tears.

"Can we have some french fries?" Hunter swiveled, taking in his surroundings. "I'm super hungry."

Tate chuckled. The EMTs exchanged amused glances. "I'm sure we can get you some french fries real soon."

The ambulance driver slammed the back doors closed. Tate stole a glance out the window. Eliana's vehicle still sat in the parking lot. He let his gaze wander until he recognized her petite figure, helping Asher and Christian load the ATVs onto the truck and trailer. The hurt in her eyes when he'd blamed her for putting the kids in danger was an image he wouldn't be able to scrub from his memory.

The engine rumbled, and the ambulance started moving. Eliana turned and watched them leave. Her gaze connected with Tate's through the window. He looked away. His phone hummed again, and he plucked the device from his pocket. Jade had called twice and sent several texts. The last message landed like a fist in his gut.

As soon as we know the twins are healthy, I'm taking them back to Boise. This was a disaster. Call me when you can.

Tate sent her a text letting her know they were on their way to the hospital and asking her to meet them there. He didn't want Willow and Hunter to leave, but at this point, there was no reason for them to stay. He could hardly blame Jade for wanting to take them home. At least then she'd know they were safe. And it wasn't like she'd trust him to find reliable childcare. Maybe he'd go back to Boise, too. Mom and Dad wouldn't be thrilled, but they'd carry on without him. After today, he didn't have a reason to stick around Hearts Bay any longer.

The rain pummeled the roof of her parents' house. Eliana huddled under a fleece blanket on the sofa. Wood popped and crackled in the fireplace. The hands on the small clock Mom kept on the side table inched toward midnight. Dad had kept the fire stoked since she'd arrived a few hours ago, drenched and sobbing. They'd fed her white chicken chili and homemade sourdough bread. She'd never been so grateful for a hot meal and a warm house.

Now her sisters were sprawled on the floor, where they'd each fallen asleep watching one of their favorite romantic comedies. Her family had rallied. Offered comfort and let her cry on their shoulders. She loved them for it.

But their kind gestures and unconditional love couldn't keep her from thinking about Tate.

Eliana stared at the television screen through a fresh wave of tears as the credits rolled. She'd tried to focus on the movie. Anything to keep her mind from replaying the horrible things he'd said to her. They'd talked about the berry picking. She'd invited Jade so she and the twins could spend quality time together. If Tate had truly believed it was too dangerous, he should've spoken up instead of giving permission.

Instead of blaming her and her *horrible* lack of judgment.

A pathetic concoction of hurt and anger churned in her gut. She pushed the blanket back and sat up. Keeping Willow and Hunter safe had always been her top priority. Accidents happened. Wasn't that what Tate had said when Willow fell and injured her mouth? Why wasn't he extending the same grace and empathy this time?

Swiping at the tears that leaked from the corners of her eyes, she leaned forward and plucked a tissue from the box on the coffee table.

Muffled voices from the kitchen drew her from the sofa. She grabbed the blanket, draped it around her shoulders, then padded into the spacious room. After Dad had finished the guest cottage out back, he'd renovated this space. Mom adored the white Shaker-style cabinets, granite countertops, brass fixtures and vintage-style lighting. Their family gatherings around the cream-colored table had eased their sorrow over the loss of Charlie and Abner.

Mom's dark eyes filled with empathy. "Hi, sweetie."

Sniffling, Eliana trudged toward the table.

Dad pulled out an empty chair. "Have a seat."

Remnants of the meal they'd enjoyed were still evident. Dirty pots and pans sat beside the sink. Plates that still needed to be loaded into the dishwasher sat in a stack. She loved that her parents had kept their ritual of sharing a cup of tea together every evening.

Selfishly, she was glad to find someone still awake. She didn't have the emotional strength to navigate this heartache on her own.

"Do you need anything else to eat?" Mom pushed back her chair. "I can reheat more chili."

"No, thanks. Please sit down." Eliana sank onto the wooden ladder-back chair beside her father and rested her head on his shoulder. "I'm fine. Just a little bit sad."

Her voice broke off. Okay, maybe more than a little sad. She dabbed at the moisture on her cheeks with the crumpled tissue. "This wasn't supposed to happen."

Dad reached over and slipped his large, strong hand into hers. "It can happen to anyone. We've all had unexpected encounters with bears. We're thankful you and the kids are safe."

"Me, too. Except I don't think Jade and Tate will ever forgive me."

"Tate will come around." Mom went to the stove and turned the kettle on, then returned to her seat at the table. "We all tend to get upset when our children are hurting or in danger."

Dad let go of her hand and reached for his mug of tea. He'd always been so good at quietly listening without judgment. Mom asked all the questions, and he absorbed the details. His calming presence helped her pour out her troubles.

"I wish he didn't blame me. I understand that Jade is upset. She has every right to be concerned, since Willow got hurt twice on my watch. But I tried to tell him that I was terrible with kids, and he—"

"Honey, no." Mom's brow furrowed. "You are not

terrible with kids. This was an accident. Willow falling after climbing on the counter was also an accident. Please don't be so hard on yourself."

Eliana cocooned tighter in the blanket she'd brought with her from the living room. "I never should've let it come to this."

Dad frowned. He shifted in his chair, his inquisitive gaze searching her face. "What do you mean?"

"From the second he walked off that ferry and I found out he wasn't married, I knew I was going to have trouble..." She hesitated and hung her head. Embarrassment crawled along her skin. "Not wanting a relationship with him. It's almost like he had a blinking warning sign—Heartbreak Ahead—and I chose to ignore it. Just plowed forward, determined to be strong."

"You're not alone," Dad said. "The Adamses and the Maddens have wrestled with this for years."

"That's what's so infuriating." Eliana battled back a fresh wave of tears. "Why can't we learn from our past mistakes? This time was no different than high school, except now there are children involved. I knew better than to open my heart, but I let him in anyway, and he rejected me."

Mom's eyes turned glassy with unshed tears. She stood and slowly circled the table, then draped her arms around Eliana. "Listen to me. We love you. This encounter with the bear was frightening for everyone. Give Tate, the children and their mother time and space to process. More importantly, be kind to yourself."

Eliana squeezed her eyes shut and tried to find comfort in her mother's words.

"You are a wonderful woman," Mom whispered, kissing the top of her head. "We love you very much."

Oh, if only she could bask in her mother's kind words and forget the pain. Wouldn't it be nice to wake up in the morning and not be swamped with regret? Except she'd fallen in love with Tate, and now she couldn't imagine her life without him. She'd put Willow and Hunter in danger and ruined her opportunity to be a part of their family. That was a mistake she was certain she'd never get over.

Chapter Twelve

Tate followed Jade and Hunter toward the security checkpoint at Orca Island's airport. Willow had insisted that he carry her. Since she wore a cast from above her knee to the base of her toes, it was hard to refuse her request. He wouldn't be allowed to go with them to the gate without a ticket, though. Christian walked behind them, pushing the wheelchair they'd borrowed.

"It's time to say goodbye, pumpkin."

"No, Daddy, no." Willow roped her arms around his neck and clung to him. "Please let me stay. I promise I'll be good."

A boulder lodged in his throat. He glanced at Jade. She hid behind her aviator sunglasses, her expression unreadable. Hunter stood beside Jade, his hand in hers, and stared at Willow. He was torn between siding with his sister and pleasing his parents. Confusion and sorrow nearly split Tate's heart wide-open.

C'mon, pull it together. He couldn't fall apart now. Not here. He kissed her forehead and rubbed her back. "Sweetie, it's time to go back to Boise. School starts soon. You'll get to meet your teacher and pick out a new backpack. Mommy's going to get you and Hunter ready to go. Aren't you excited?"

Man, he was blabbering. Willow saw right through his ploy to distract her.

"I want to stay here with you. Eliana can teach me school."

Ouch. He forced a gentle smile. "That's not going to work. Eliana's not a teacher."

"She can teach me at her house. Some mommies do that." Willow clung to him as he tried to set her on her feet, then remembered that wasn't an option. Christian inched closer with the wheelchair.

Jade sighed. "That's enough, Willow. We need to go. It's almost time to board."

Tate transferred Willow into the wheelchair. As soon as he straightened, Hunter jerked his hand free from Jade's and clung to Tate's legs. "Please come with us, Daddy."

Jade whipped off her sunglasses. A vein bulged in the center of her forehead. "This is ridiculous. You two are making a huge scene. Get in line. Now."

Christian and Tate exchanged glances.

"When you get on the plane, I'll buy you Wi-Fi. You each have your own iPad right here." Jade patted her leather handbag. "Doesn't that sound fun?"

Willow slumped in her wheelchair and glared at Jade. Hunter tightened his grip on Tate's legs. *Oh, my.* This was going to be excruciating. He gently pried Hunter's hands loose.

"Please, no," Hunter wailed.

How could one little boy's voice get so loud? Heat crawled up Tate's neck as Hunter clung tighter. Panic zipped white-hot through his veins. People were watching his family melt down in the middle of the airport. How was he supposed to force his children to leave when they desperately wanted to stay?

"Hunter, it's my turn for a goodbye hug," Christian said. "You wouldn't leave without saying goodbye to your favorite uncle, would you?"

Hunter took a breath and studied Christian. "Will you lift me way high up?"

Christian frowned. "How high?"

"Way high up." Hunter let go of Tate's legs and reached his arm up in the air. "To the ceiling."

"I really don't think I can. You've gotten so strong this summer, helping your dad and grandpa and playing outside. I'm afraid your muscles are too big and I can't do it. Sorry." Christian shrugged and stepped toward Willow. "I'm only handing out tiny hugs today."

"What's a tiny hug?" Hunter's brow furrowed. "Is that really a thing?"

Jade and Tate both laughed. Thankfully, Christian had smoothed the tension with his goofy sense of humor.

"I'll show you." Willow giggled as Christian touched the top of his head to hers then patted her shoulder. "That's a tiny hug."

"But I want a big giant one." Hunter's eyes gleamed with anticipation. "You have to try."

"Okay, I'll try one time, but I'm pretty sure your muscles are way too big and I can't lift you." Christian leaned down and slid his hands under Hunter's armpits. He grunted and grimaced, pretending like Hunter weighed a thousand pounds.

"Do it. Lift me now." Hunter's giggle bubbled up, drawing smiles from the people waiting in line at security.

With a loud roar, Christian raised him up and jogged around the corridor, flying Hunter like an airplane.

Willow sniffed, then smiled up at Tate and slipped her hand into his.

Tate leaned over and kissed the top of her head again. "Uncle Christian's fun, isn't he?"

"I'm going to miss you, Daddy. Please bring Eliana with you when you come home."

"Okay, now it's really time to go." Jade turned and called, "Come on, Hunter. We've got to get in line."

Tate ran his hand over his face. "I don't know, sweetie. That's not a promise I can make."

"But you have to try," Willow said, repeating her brother's plea. "I know you can make her happy, Daddy. Just try."

She was a determined little thing. He squeezed her hand, then pulled away. She reached up and formed his cheeks into a smile. "Don't be sad. Smile. Because Eliana likes it when you smile."

"Really? How do you know?"

Willow shrugged. "I just do. When you smile, then she smiles, and everybody's happy."

Did he just get relationship advice from his five-year-old daughter?

He had known how to make Eliana happy once upon a time, but he'd said some harsh things after he'd found her and the kids. What if she didn't forgive him? He wasn't even sure he could forgive himself. Wow, he'd been cruel.

Hunter and Christian returned. The gate agent announced early boarding for their flight.

"I'll see you soon, Willow. We'll be together again before you know it." He tugged on one of her curls. "Be good. I love you."

She clutched her backpack in her lap. "I love you, too, Daddy."

"Hunter, give me one more hug. Tiny or big, it doesn't matter." Tate held his arms wide, and Hunter fell into them. His body trembled. Tate kissed his forehead and savored the little-boy scents of sugar and laundry soap. "I love you very much."

"I know," Hunter whispered. "I love you, Daddy. Please come home soon."

Tate squeezed his eyes shut. "I promise by the time you start kindergarten, I'll be there to take you. That's less than two weeks from now."

"Hunter, c'mon. Willow gets to board first." Jade grabbed the handles on the wheelchair. "I'll text you when we land. Thanks for everything."

"You're welcome." Tate stood with Christian and watched until they were through the security checkpoint. Their gate was the first one, and Hunter looked back and waved one more time. Tate waved. If they didn't hurry and get on that plane, he was going to melt into a puddle.

When they were out of sight, he felt the weight of Christian's stare. "Whatever you're thinking, man, lay it on me."

"There's still time to make this right."

"Make what right? I'm not getting on that plane. Jade wants to have the kids with her."

"I'm not talking about getting on a plane. This has nothing to do with Jade." Christian nudged him on the shoulder. "Dude, you're free. No parental responsibilities, so go see Eliana. Apologize and tell her you can't survive without her. Make her *smile*."

"You heard Willow's advice, huh?"

"Sure did." Christian grinned. "And you should listen to your daughter."

"I have one more stop to make first."

Christian's brow furrowed. "Who?"

"Pop."

Surprise flashed in his brother's eyes. "You're going to speak to Pop about your relationship with a Madden?"

"To be honest, it's a conversation I should've had with him a long time ago." He pulled his keys from his pocket. "Thanks again for your help. And your advice."

"Anytime." Christian clapped him on the back. "Now go be brave."

Tate turned and jogged toward the exit. He hoped and prayed that his grandfather would give his blessing to put an end to this conflict that festered between their families—and that Eliana would speak to him.

A few minutes later, after he'd checked in at the front desk, he pushed through the back doors of the senior living center. An incredible view of the mountains sporting their rich green summer foliage greeted him. Containers of orange, pink and yellow poppies bloomed on either side of the concrete path. Birds chirped in the trees nearby. He stopped in the middle of the concrete path and surveyed the courtyard. The woman at the front desk had assured him Pop was out here. She said he spent almost every sunny afternoon outside dozing in his wheelchair.

A familiar deep voice and the squirrels nattering drew his attention toward a man sitting near the base of a spruce tree. Tate smiled. His grandfather sat parked in his wheelchair with a faded quilt draped over his legs. He had a plastic bag in his lap. Whatever he tossed on the ground, the squirrels gobbled up. Tate cut across the grass, waving at a couple of family friends chatting nearby.

"Hey, Pop." Tate stopped beside his grandfather's wheelchair. "Keeping the squirrels happy today?"

Pop tipped his bald head up and squinted. "Tate, what are you doing here?"

"I came by to see how you're doing."

Pop shifted in his chair, then chucked another handful of sunflower seeds on the ground. "So this is a casual visit?"

Tate rubbed his palm across the back of his neck. "Yep."

"Pull up a chair. By the way, you're a terrible liar."

Tate pushed out a nervous laugh as he dragged a plastic lawn chair over.

"I'm doing fine, but you've clearly got something on your mind." Pop readjusted the quilt on his lap. "Give me the short version. It's almost time for my nap. Besides, your father's already been here and told me his version of the story."

"My dad's already been here? What story did he tell you?"

Pop's gaze sharpened, and his bushy white eyebrows furrowed. "The same story we're always telling in this family. The one that revolves around a Madden."

Tate sighed and leaned forward, propping his elbows on his knees. He studied his clasped hands. Eliana's pained expression flashed in his head again. "I messed up, Pop."

His grandfather crumpled the empty sunflower seed bag in his hand. "We all make mistakes. There's still time to make things right."

"I blamed Eliana for an accident, something that wasn't her fault. I was mean, too."

"Have you apologized?"

Tate shook his head then looked away.

"What are you waiting for?"

He hesitated. His mouth ran dry. What was he waiting for? Permission? "I'm ashamed of my behavior, but I'm also worried that you and Dad will never forgive me if I marry a Madden."

A heavy silence hung between them. Pop reached over and placed his gnarled hand on Tate's arm. "Look at me, boy."

Tate dragged his gaze to meet Pop's. Those fierce blue eyes still made him squirm. "I'm going to tell you the same thing I told your father. Sell that land. All of it. Put an end to the nonsense. Our families have gone toe-to-toe over this for far too long."

Tate stared at him. He didn't know what to say. Yeah, he'd come looking for advice, but he hadn't allowed himself to hope that Pop would be the first to campaign for peace between their families.

"What's the matter? You don't think an old man's capable of forgiveness?"

"That's not... I didn't—"

"Now go on and give that Madden girl whatever she wants. Take it from me—if you love her, you'd better tell her before it's too late."

"Thanks, Pop." Tate clapped his grandfather on the shoulder. "Take care, okay? I'll stop by again soon."

"Did you hear me? I said, 'Go on.'" Pop pointed toward the building. "I need a nap."

Tate swallowed a laugh. "Yes, sir."

He cut long strides across the courtyard, then broke

into a jog. Pop was right. Their families had sown division for far too long. He could change all that. Starting today. If only Eliana would give him an opportunity to make things right.

They were gone.

Tate had left again, just like she knew he would.

Eliana stared at the photo Rylee had texted less than an hour ago. With trembling fingers, she touched the image of Tate, Jade and the twins going inside the airport. Even though Jade had remarried, they were still a family of four, and this snapshot only reminded her that she didn't belong. They had a well-established life back in Boise. Memories of Willow zipping down the sidewalk on her scooter and Hunter's belly laugh bubbling up as he ran across the playground with Cameron made her cry harder.

She missed them so much that it physically hurt.

The sad-face emoji Rylee had sent along with the photo didn't even begin to describe her sorrow. Eliana dabbed at the fresh tears on her cheeks with a crumpled tissue.

If only she'd tried harder. Given more careful thought to that hike before she led children into the woods to pick berries right smack in the middle of bear country. She deleted the photo, then tossed her phone on the sofa and burrowed deeper under the blanket.

Why had she been so careless? Tate had every reason to be upset with her. Jade, too. She'd risked the lives of their precious children, and it broke her heart to think about how frightened they must've been.

Wallowing on her sofa hadn't helped. Or changed her circumstances. Rylee's photo confirmed her worst fears—he'd left and there wasn't going to be a good-bye. She reached for her laptop on the coffee table and let the blanket drop to the floor. A few months ago, she would've laughed if anyone who knew her well tried to tell her she'd be pondering a major life change by the end of the summer. Now the idea of changing her plans filled her with equal parts excitement and trepidation. She hesitated, gnawing on her thumbnail, then refreshed the webpage. Information about radiology technician programs in Idaho filled the screen.

This morning, fueled by a fresh wave of optimism—plus a moose tracks mocha hand-delivered by Annie—Eliana had revisited the application process. But the text from Rylee and the realization that Tate and the kids were leaving the island without saying goodbye brought on a fresh wave of hurt. She'd abandoned the application without even finishing the first half.

Now her fingers hovered over the track pad. Maybe she should delete the information she'd just supplied. If Tate didn't want her in Idaho, then she might as well apply to a program closer to home. Mom's ongoing health issues meant she'd be making frequent trips to Seattle. Maybe she'd apply to programs there. Or try distance learning and stay on the island. She'd need to find a new job, though.

A knock at the door wrenched her from her internal debate.

Who could that be? Her family had promised to leave her be today, and the only friend she'd wanted to see had already stopped by. A quick glimpse in the oval mirror mounted on the living room wall earned a grimace. Should she answer the door wearing flannel pajamas patterned with Christmas lights and a gray T-shirt that had seen better days? She poked her finger through the hole near the shirt's hem. Classy.

Her visitor knocked again.

"Coming." She plucked her anorak from the hall closet and slipped it on, then dragged her fingers through her tangled hair. Whoever stood on her porch would just have to be okay with the fact that she was wearing yesterday's eye makeup.

She hesitated, stealing a peek through the sidelight before she turned the dead bolt.

Tate stood on her porch.

She gasped. Had Rylee played a prank with that photo? *No.* Her little sister had a great sense of humor and loved to tease others, but she wasn't mean.

Eliana unlocked the door, then turned the knob slowly. "Tate?" She blinked against the brightness. There wasn't a single cloud in the brilliant blue sky. The midmorning sunshine made the boughs on the evergreen trees and the carpet of grass on her lawn seem more vibrant than normal.

"Hey." His eyes searched her face. "I'm glad I caught you at home."

"I thought you left."

His tentative half smile sent her heart into orbit. One look at that boyish curve of his lips and she almost forgot those harsh words they'd exchanged. Almost.

Yes, he'd accused her of endangering his children's lives. But hadn't she been equally cruel when she'd dismissed his bold invitation to start over in Idaho?

He shoved his hands in the back pockets of his jeans. Those incredible blue eyes searched her face.

She propped one shoulder against the door frame. Why was he here? Did the twins leave? She resisted the temptation to look past him and check if they were waiting in the truck.

"Do you have a few minutes to talk? Sorry I stopped by unannounced, but I wasn't sure you'd let me in if I called ahead." He glanced down and scuffed the edge of his brown boot against the bristles on her doormat. "I have quite a few things I need to apologize for."

"Me, too," she said, her voice barely more than a whisper. Then she stepped back and motioned for him to come inside.

"Would you like something to drink? Water? Coffee?"

They stood in her entryway, and he shook his head. "No. I—I need to tell you this now." Pausing, he pushed his fingers through his hair.

She clutched at the lapels of her jacket. Her breath bottled in her chest. What did he need to say?

"I'm sorry. I know my words carry little weight since my actions have been so hurtful. My family has crushed your plans, and I'm ashamed of our behavior."

She licked her lips and started to speak. The words wouldn't come.

He kept going. "I should have brought Willow and Hunter over so that they could say goodbye. They've both asked for you several times, and Willow really wants to show you her cast."

"I wish I could see it."

Tate's features pinched. "The tree falling on the café, my parents' quest to change zoning laws to meet their own needs, Jade showing up… You have no idea how much I regret the way these last several days have gone. The last several weeks, really. I thought if I tried harder, had one more conversation, went on one more fishing charter, that my parents would somehow change their minds. But in the end, it didn't work."

His earnestness softened the last of her anger. Her arms ached to hold him. To be held. She clutched her jacket lapels tighter, determined to hear him out.

"Our families have argued over the same issues for decades. No matter what happens next, if you accept my apology or you never want to speak to me again, I wanted you to know that I'm sorry. The way my parents and I have treated you is inexcusable. I hope someday you can forgive me. Forgive all of us."

This time the words came easily. Without hesitation. "You're forgiven."

His eyes widened and he shifted from one foot to the other, his hands braced on his hips. "That was fast."

"If I've learned anything this summer, it's that a grudge is a poisonous thing. It consumes entire families. I almost let it destroy the best relationship I've ever known." She paused, letting her words sink in, and gathered the courage to say more. "I'm sorry, Tate. The other night at my parents' house, I was thoughtless. You deserved a proper answer, and I let my fear get in the way."

"Given how selfish I've been, and the way my parents have treated you, I don't blame you for proceeding with caution. You have every right to tell me to get lost."

Her throat tightened. "But that's not what I want."

In true Tate fashion, he took the first step and bridged the gap between them. "Good, because that's not what I want, either."

Their gazes locked. A hum of awareness zinged in the air. He reached for her, his fingertips skimming along the sleeves of her jacket until he gently cupped her cheeks with his hands.

"Wait." She clasped his upper arms, forcing herself to concentrate on what she needed to say and not the wonderful sensation of his callused hands on her skin.

He searched her face. "What's wrong? Tell me."

"Not everyone who loves us will support our relationship. If we're going to be together, how will we navigate that?"

"We'll tell them what we should've a long time ago."

"What's that?" she whispered, inching closer, the anticipation of his kiss sending a pleasant tremor through her abdomen.

"That we're meant to be, and we don't need their approval. This summer you've reminded me that my world is not complete without you. I am so sorry for the terrible things I've said. Your forgiveness is a gift I don't deserve. Willow, Hunter and I are so grateful for everything you've done for us. I love you, Eliana."

She leaned into the warmth of his caress. Was this really happening?

"I love you, too," she said, letting herself get lost in the unplumbed depths of his smoldering blue eyes.

Then his mouth was on hers. He loved her. Tate Adams loved *her*.

He splayed his hands across her lower back and pulled her closer. She responded to his touch, linking her hands behind his neck and tunneling her fingers through his hair. The familiar fragrance of his aftershave, the safe cocoon of his embrace and his humble words echoing in her ears chased away all her concerns. She thought of nothing else except the two of them, wrapped in each other's arms, surrounded by the hope of forever.

Epilogue

Eliana circled the crowded parking lot a second time, scouting for a vacant spot. Tate had asked her to meet him near their new favorite restaurant, an upscale place that made their own pasta in-house. Her mouth watered just thinking about the scrumptious food. Too bad every person with a car and a driver's license had decided to spend the evening in downtown Boise.

She hated to keep Tate waiting, especially tonight. Her last class had gone over, then she'd rushed back to her apartment near the university. Now she was running late because she'd spent a few extra minutes on her hair and makeup. It had only been eight months since she had moved to Boise to be closer to Tate and the twins.

Often, they tried to include the twins in their outings, but this weekend the kids were with Rex and Tammy. Tate's family had sold their waterfront property, closed their fishing charter business and bought a lake house in Idaho just two hours from Boise. Willow and Hunter loved visiting their grandparents at their new home. They'd begged for one last adventure before the fall temperatures arrived shortly and put an end to their lake time for the year.

Thankfully the twins' absence meant a special dinner for just her and Tate. After a busy week of classes and a glimpse at a grueling semester as she worked toward becoming a radiology technician, she was eager for a romantic dinner. Especially one at a restaurant more suitable for adults than six-year-olds. Candlelight, delicious pasta and lingering over dessert with her man—the recipe for an ideal Friday night.

Finally, on her third lap around the lot, when she was about to give up and look for a space in the parking garage two blocks down the street, a sedan backed out of a nearby spot.

"Woohoo!" She punched the air with her fist, then pressed the brake and turned on her blinker. Drumming her fingertips on the steering wheel, she hummed along to a song on the radio while she waited for the space to clear. A text message arrived on her phone, releasing the familiar muffled chime from the depths of her handbag. Probably Tate wondering where she was.

She parked and turned off the engine, then checked her hair and lipstick in the visor mirror one last time before retrieving her phone and checking the messages. Rylee had sent her a photo, which wasn't unusual. The girl snapped pics of all sorts of adventures multiple times a week and eagerly shared them. This time, the photo featured a gorgeous shot of Hearts Bay's waterfront. A stunning new hotel filled the frame, complete with a Grand Opening banner draped across the main entrance.

Eliana smiled. The café and the building that once stood next door were nothing but memories now. She missed her old life sometimes. But the developer who'd bought the property from Rex and Tammy had proceeded with great care. The new hotel, which evidently had two wonderful ballrooms to host receptions and other special events, looked incredible. Eliana couldn't help but wonder what all the older generations of Maddens and Adamses would think if they could see "their" waterfront now.

She hopped out of the car and crossed the parking lot. Her heels clicked on the pavement as she hurried down the sidewalk. The warm evening breeze swirled around her bare shoulders. She drew in a deep breath. City life had been quite an adjustment. The pace, the traffic, the noises—hardly anything in Idaho resembled her comfortable routine back home in Hearts Bay. Some days all the change felt overwhelming. But she was thriving.

And Tate was here.

That made the upheaval more than worthwhile. They saw each other as often as possible. His reputation as a trustworthy home builder had allowed him to strike out on his own—he no longer had to work for Jade's family. And even though it wasn't always easy interacting with Jade, Eliana adored spending time with Willow and Hunter. They were healthy and happy. She'd had a ball all summer, going swimming and hiking with them and playing at the park. They already had a long list of fall activities they'd invited her to attend.

She rounded the corner of the building, and her steps faltered. Tate stood outside the restaurant dressed in dark blue slacks, a crisp white button-down shirt and brown leather oxfords. He grinned, and her heart expanded. She hurried to meet him. Sure, she missed her parents, her sisters and Annie, but as she drew closer and Tate presented her with a bouquet of red roses, she knew she was exactly where she was supposed to be.

"These are for you."

"Thank you. They're beautiful." The paper crinkled in her hands as she took the flowers and tucked them in the crook of her arm. Then she pressed up on her tiptoes and brushed her lips against his.

He kissed her gently, then leaned back, his eyes sweeping over her. "You look amazing."

"Thank you." She twirled in a quick circle, letting the skirt flow out from her bare legs.

He took her hand in his and led her down a flagstone path beside the restaurant. "Have I mentioned that you look stunning when you wear that shade of green?"

"Maybe once or twice, but tell me again."

His husky laugh filled the air. She'd never get tired of hearing that sound. "Wait, where are we going?"

She took in the beautiful flowers spilling from oversize planters and the well-manicured grass stretching beside a canopy of leafy green trees. Vintage Edison-style lights on black strings crisscrossed a pergola. Romantic classical music played from a speaker she couldn't quite locate. The people who'd filled the sidewalks in front of the restaurant seemed to have disappeared. Only she and Tate remained in the center of this breathtaking oasis.

"Tate?"

Somehow while she'd been admiring their surroundings, he'd let go of her hand. She turned and found him behind her. "What's going—"

Oh, my. He'd dropped to one knee on the pavement. The crescendo of classical music, birds chirping overhead and the aromas of tomatoes and garlic all faded into the background. All she could see and think about was Tate's chiseled jaw, the emotion swimming in his eyes and his tentative smile as he reached for her hand again.

"Eliana, I knew when I went back home last summer, that my life would never be the same. I am so grateful that God has brought us back together. You are a gift and an abundant blessing."

He paused, fighting to keep his composure.

Her vision blurred with unshed tears.

"I wasn't sure I could ever trust my heart with someone again. But your love has changed me. I am a better father and a better man because of you. That's why I can't imagine a future that doesn't include you." He held out a velvet box and opened it. "Eliana, will you marry me?"

She gasped, the tears spilling over as she clutched her flowers in one hand and extended her left. "Yes!"

The next few minutes were a blur as he slid the ring on her finger, then stood and pulled her into his arms. "I love you so much," she said, tucking her head under his chin.

He pulled back, his fingertips caressing her upper arms as his eyes searched her face. "I love you, too."

They stood in the not-so-secret garden, kissing, as applause erupted from somewhere behind them. Then footsteps pounded and suddenly Eliana's sisters enveloped them in a giant group hug, laughing through their tears.

"What in the world?" Eliana found Tate's eyes through the tangle of arms and radiant smiles of the people she loved most.

He winked. "You didn't think I'd leave your sisters out of this, did you?"

"And you didn't think we'd let him leave us out, did you?" Rylee teased, pulling Eliana in for a hug.

"No, of course not," Eliana said. "But that picture. You texted me from Hearts Bay a few minutes ago."

"Oh, I took that last week." Rylee waggled her eyebrows. "That was just to throw you off the path. Tate was worried that you knew he'd propose tonight. Were you surprised?"

"Absolutely."

Rylee took a ridiculous bow. "Then my work here is done."

While her sisters clutched her left hand in theirs and praised Tate for the gorgeous diamond solitaire he'd selected, Tate managed to break through the chaos and kiss her again. "I can't wait for you to be my wife."

"I'm going to make you the happiest man alive, Tate Adams."

* * * * *

*If you enjoyed this Home to Hearts Bay story
by Heidi McCahan, be sure to pick up
the first book in this series,* An Alaskan Secret,
available now from Love Inspired!

Dear Reader,

One of the most frequently asked questions authors receive is how we get ideas for our books. For me, my ideas often come from observations I've made in my everyday life. Whether I'm chatting with friends over coffee, attending a family reunion or catching up on news from my hometown, snippets of conversation and interesting details often spark a new story idea.

It's only in the writing process that I discover the story isn't just for all of you to enjoy, but that God often has something important He wants to teach me as well. I have found that overcoming painful situations and learning to forgive and love one another can be quite challenging. Perhaps you can relate. Eliana, Tate and their families are not real, yet the lessons they had to learn in this story are applicable to our real-world circumstances. My hope for you, reader friends, is that you will run to the one who loves us unconditionally. May you find courage and draw strength from the words of our Lord, who promises He always hears our prayers and never leaves us.

Thank you for supporting Christian fiction and telling your friends how much you enjoy our books. I'd love to connect with you. You can find me online: https://www.facebook.com/heidimccahan/, http://heidimccahan.com/ or https://www.instagram.com/heidimccahan.author. For news about book releases and sales, sign up for my author newsletter: http://www.subscribepage.com/heidimccahan-newoptin.

Until next time,
Heidi

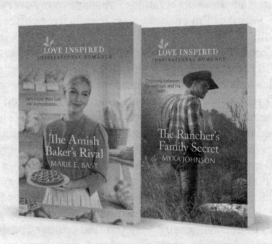

Get 4 FREE REWARDS!

We'll send you 2 FREE Books plus 2 FREE Mystery Gifts.

FREE
Value Over
$20

Both the **Love Inspired®** and **Love Inspired® Suspense** series feature compelling
novels filled with inspirational romance, faith, forgiveness, and hope.

YES! Please send me 2 FREE novels from the Love Inspired or Love Inspired
Suspense series and my 2 FREE gifts (gifts are worth about $10 retail). After
receiving them, if I don't wish to receive any more books, I can return the shipping
statement marked "cancel." If I don't cancel, I will receive 6 brand-new Love
Inspired Larger-Print books or Love Inspired Suspense Larger-Print books every
month and be billed just $5.99 each in the U.S. or $6.24 each in Canada. That
is a savings of at least 17% off the cover price. It's quite a bargain! Shipping
and handling is just 50¢ per book in the U.S. and $1.25 per book in Canada.*
I understand that accepting the 2 free books and gifts places me under no
obligation to buy anything. I can always return a shipment and cancel at any time.
The free books and gifts are mine to keep no matter what I decide.

Choose one: ☐ **Love Inspired**   ☐ **Love Inspired Suspense**
                Larger-Print   **Larger-Print**
                (122/322 IDN GNWC)   (107/307 IDN GNWN)

Name (please print)

Address   Apt. #

City   State/Province   Zip/Postal Code

Email: Please check this box ☐ if you would like to receive newsletters and promotional emails from Harlequin Enterprises ULC and
its affiliates. You can unsubscribe anytime.

Mail to the **Harlequin Reader Service:**
IN U.S.A.: P.O. Box 1341, Buffalo, NY 14240-8531
IN CANADA: P.O. Box 603, Fort Erie, Ontario L2A 5X3

Want to try 2 free books from another series? Call **1-800-873-8635** or visit www.ReaderService.com.

*Terms and prices subject to change without notice. Prices do not include sales taxes, which will be charged (if applicable) based
on your state or country of residence. Canadian residents will be charged applicable taxes. Offer not valid in Quebec. This offer is
limited to one order per household. Books received may not be as shown. Not valid for current subscribers to the Love Inspired or
Love Inspired Suspense series. All orders subject to approval. Credit or debit balances in a customer's account(s) may be offset by
any other outstanding balance owed by or to the customer. Please allow 4 to 6 weeks for delivery. Offer available while quantities last.

Your Privacy—Your information is being collected by Harlequin Enterprises ULC, operating as Harlequin Reader Service. For a
complete summary of the information we collect, how we use this information and to whom it is disclosed, please visit our privacy notice
located at corporate.harlequin.com/privacy-notice. From time to time we may also exchange your personal information with reputable
third parties. If you wish to opt out of this sharing of your personal information, please visit readerservice.com/consumerschoice or
call 1-800-873-8635. **Notice to California Residents**—Under California law, you have specific rights to control and access your data.
For more information on these rights and how to exercise them, visit corporate.harlequin.com/california-privacy.

LIRLIS22